D1298675

The Big Domino in the Sky

The Big Domino in the Sky

and Other Atheistic Tales

Michael Martin

author of the acclaimed *Case Against Christianity*

Prometheus Books
59 John Glenn Drive
Amherst, NewYork 14228-2197

Published 1996 by Prometheus Books

00 99 98 97 96 5 4 3 2 1

Library of Congress Cataloging-in-Publication Data

Martin, Michael, 1932–
The big domino in the sky / by Michael Martin.
p. cm.
ISBN 1–57392–111–4 (pbk. : alk. paper)
1. Fantastic fiction American. 2. Historical fiction, American. 3. Atheists—Fiction. 4. Atheism—Fiction. I. Title.
PS3563.A72635B54 1996
813'54—dc20 96–34925
CIP

Printed in the United States of America on acid-free paper

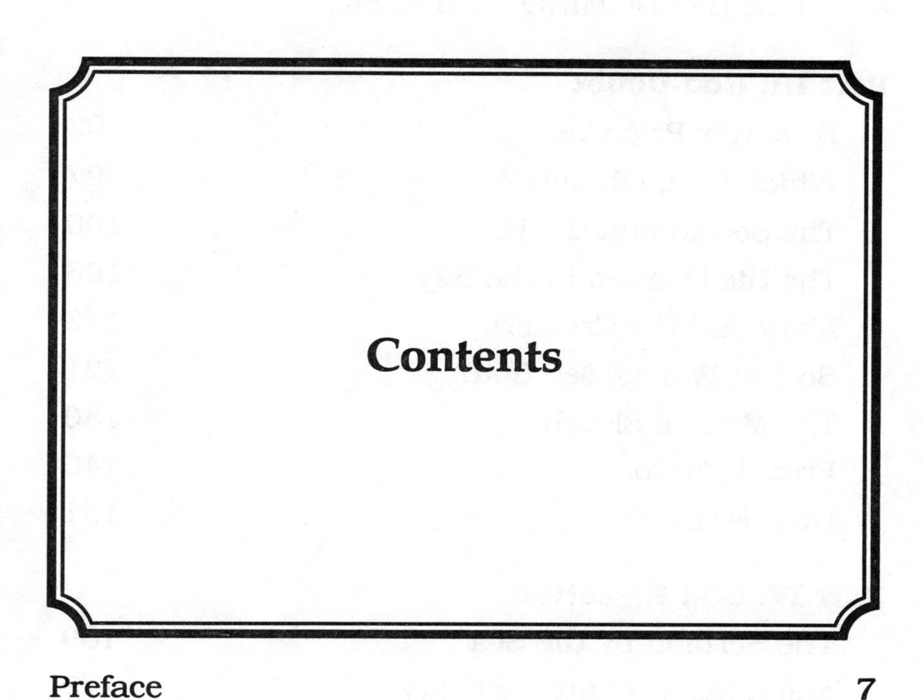

Contents

Preface 7

Prologue 11

Part I: Beginnings

Definitions 21

The Preacher with No Name 25

Letters from Lois 29

Are You an Atheist and Don't Know It? 45

Part II: God-Fall

Definitions 55

An Interview with Gustav Miller 57

Did I Cause Smerdyakov's Suicide? 64

Miller's Inferno 71

Part III: God-Doubt

Howard's Prologue 93
Which God, Oh Lord? 97
The Sermon on the Hill 100
The Big Domino in the Sky 106
Mary and the Creators 113
So You Wanna See God? 121
The Miracle Sleuth 130
Frenchy's Con 146
Dear Mom 151

Part IV: God-Rejection

The Sermon by the Sea 169
Mary, Mary, Quite Contrary 179
The Death of Beneficent Ben 188
God for a Day! 191
The Free Will Improvement Project 201
The Satanic Curses 223
Sergeant Allen and Professor Hick 230

Epilogue: God-Free at Last! 241

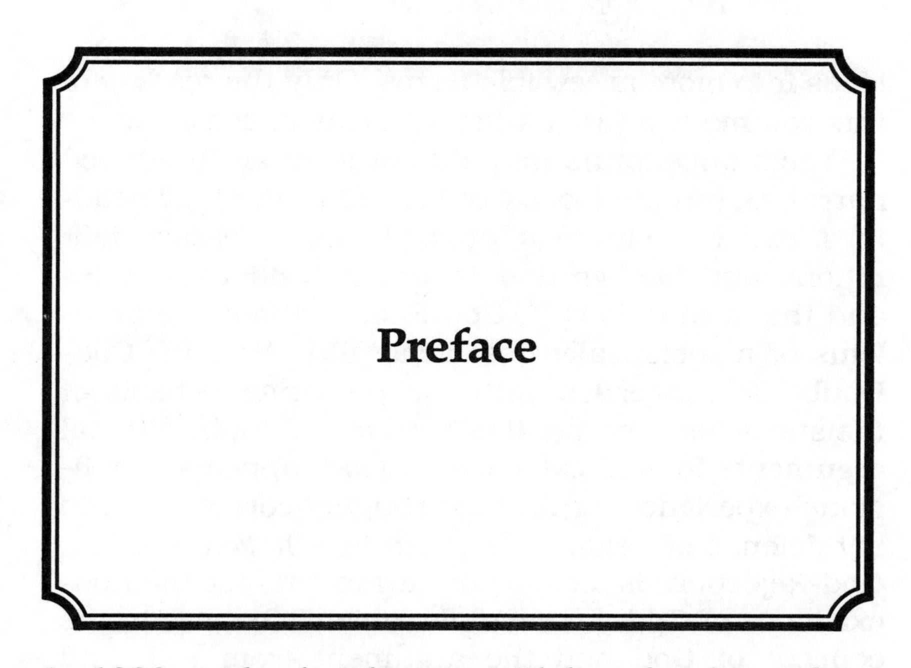

Preface

In 1990 my book *Atheism: A Philosophical Justification* was published by Temple University Press. Intended for professional philosophers and bristling with sophisticated arguments that were couched in the symbolism of modal logic and probability theory, it was long—over five hundred pages—and technical. Even some professional philosophers complained that it was hard to read. My wife, herself a professional philosopher, realizing the problem, suggested that I write a popular book on atheism. Her suggestion appealed to me, but I had previously written only for professional philosophers. Could I do it? Then I recalled that I had told bedtime stories to my sons when they were young. Could I reclaim my storytelling ability for a different purpose? Could I create stories that would illustrate the basic tenets of atheism? I thought I should try to translate atheistic ideas into more accessible terms. Only the readers of this volume can judge whether I was successful.

The stories found here do not form an integrated narrative, but are loosely organized under four headings. Part I, Beginnings, provides the necessary definitions and background to understand the stories and the author. Part II, God-Fall, is about the problems of a theistically based morality. Part III, God-Doubt, is concerned with the problematic basis of theistic belief, whether it is in terms of the traditional arguments for the existence of God, appeals to religious experience, or faith. It roughly corresponds to my defense of negative atheism in *Atheism.* Part III, God-Rejection, is focused on arguments for the nonexistence of God, for example, inconsistencies in the concept of God and the argument from evil, and roughly corresponds to my defense of positive atheism in *Atheism.* The Epilogue discusses what an atheistic society might be like. As a reader will soon discover, the categories—God-Fall, God-Doubt, God-Rejection, and God-Free, are taken from one series of stories in the book concerning an imaginary twenty-second-century atheistic movement that has a charismatic preacher, a set of quasi-religious doctrines, and a privileged text. Readers should not infer that I approve of, let alone recommend, this form of atheism. The stories are meant merely to illustrate one form that atheism can take.

With a few exceptions, all characters in this book are purely fictitious and any resemblance to actual persons living or dead is purely coincidental. Professor Hick is a real person, but the story in which he appears is fictional. The character Reverend William Paley in "Mary, Mary, Quite Contrary" was a real person, although the story itself is obviously fictional.

"The Big Domino in the Sky" is purely fictional, although my step-grandfather, a character in this story, was a real person and held the basic beliefs attributed to him in this story as well as in the story "Letters from Lois." The stories "Letters from Lois," "Did I Cause Smerdyakov's Suicide?" and "The Satanic Curses," in which I appear as a character, are purely fictional. I am indebted to my wife for the idea for this book as well as for her critical comments. I am grateful to my sons for providing me with storytelling experience, and to Cecile Watters for her invaluable help in editing the manuscript.

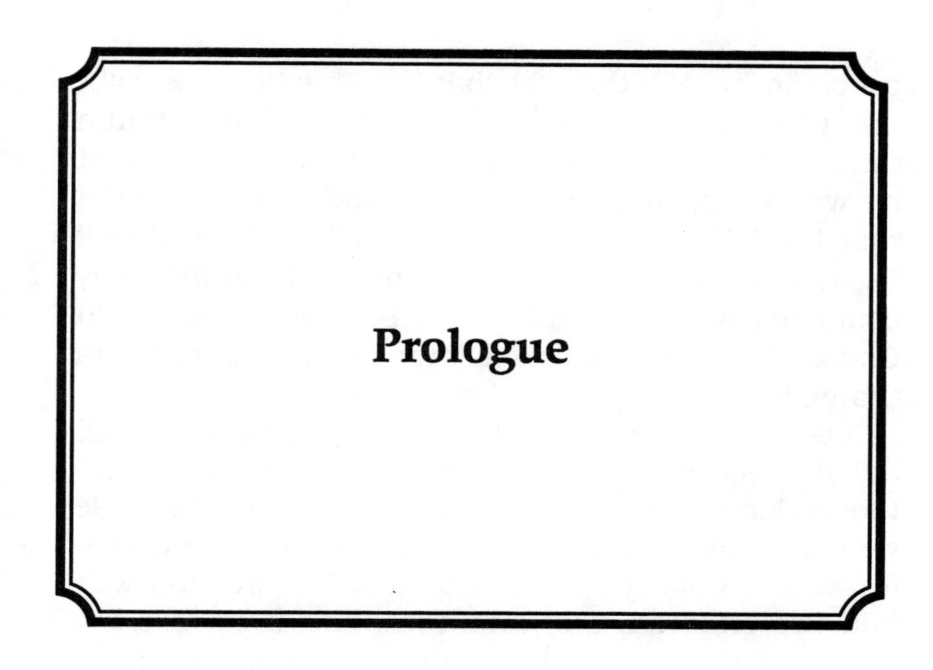

Prologue

I recall the night many years ago when Tim and Tom were young and wanted their usual story. I told them that the story that night would have to be abbreviated since I had lots of work to do. Sitting on a bed, I said that I would tell them "an anti-fairy tale." Naturally they wanted to know what this was. Ignoring their question, I suggested that they listen. I narrated a story about how once upon a time there was a little boy who did not believe in fairies, brownies, goblins, Santa Claus, leprechauns, the Easter Bunny, or God. He did not say his prayers and did not go to church. His grandfather, whom the little boy loved very much, and who also did not believe in fairies, brownies, goblins, Santa Claus, leprechauns, the Easter Bunny, or God, talked to him about the nonexistence of God and taught him many things. I explained to them how people in his city thought that the little boy was right not to believe in fairies, brownies, goblins, Santa Claus, leprechauns, and the Easter Bunny, but that he was wrong not to believe in God. Some thought that the little boy was wicked and would go to Hell because he did not believe in God. But the little boy could not see much difference between believing in God and believing in fairies, brownies, goblins, Santa Claus, leprechauns, and the Easter Bunny.

I went on to say that when the boy grew up he still did not believe in fairies, brownies, goblins, Santa Claus, leprechauns, the Easter Bunny, or God. He went to a big school in the East and became a professor of philosophy and married. He and his wife had two children, Tim and Tom, and lived in a big white house on a hill. He wrote a big book about not believing in God and they lived happily ever after. I kissed them "Good night" and was about the turn out the light. But before I could, they voiced their objections. Tom complained that my anti-fairy tale was not a "real story." Energetically bouncing on the bed, Tim said that they wanted a story about space travel or ghosts. Tom also objected that my story was true and he demanded a story that was "pretend." Tim wanted to know if the story was indeed true. I assured them that the story was true in part. I explained that the little boy in the story was me and Tim and Tom were them, but that I had not yet written a big book about not believing in God, although perhaps someday I would.

Now they were both bouncing on the bed, protesting that the story was too short and that in any case they were not sleepy. They were right on both counts. The story was the shortest I had ever told them, and I had never seen them more wide awake. I promised

I would tell them a story about a leprechaun who became a Member of Parliament. I did tell them such a story, just as on other nights I created stories about fairies, brownies, space monsters, boys with magic powers, and the like. These stories were all invented. I never constructed a story about God, although Tim and Tom, like the little boy in the anti-fairy tale, believed that God was pretend too. I am not sure why I never made up a story about God. Perhaps I thought that although God was make-believe it was serious make-believe. Billions of people really believe in God; relatively few believed in the entities and powers postulated in my bedtime stories.

Although my short anti-fairy tale was not completely true at the time I first related it, it is now. I wrote a big book on nonbelief and until recently we lived in a big white house on the top of a hill. Since Tim and Tom are now grown-ups, I needed a new audience for my stories. So I wrote another book in the form of stories based on the big book, not in order to entertain children, but to present the case for atheism in an enjoyable way. In fact, you are just starting to read it! Whether Tim and Tom would like it I don't know.

In any case, here are the main characters:

The Eighteenth Century

The Creators	A group of finite but powerful, morally imperfect, supernatural beings who create universes

Mary Taylor	A young English woman interested in philosophy and theology
Rev. William Paley	A theologian, advocate of the Argument from Design
Mr. and Mrs. Taylor	Mary's parents

The Nineteenth Century

Smerdyakov	The epileptic servant of Fyodor Pavlovitch Karamazov in Dostoyevsky's novel *The Brothers Karamazov,* who advocated the view that if God does not exist, everything is permitted

The Twentieth Century

Michael Martin	A philosophy professor at Boston University, father of Tim and Tom
Louis (Lou) Young	Step-grandfather of Michael
Satan	The Devil, in the guise of a European gentleman
Ann Larson	New York writer, mother of Bobby, student of judo
Robert (Bobby) Larson	A sophomore at Harvard University

Paul and Joe	Bobby's roommates at Dunster House
Dr. Frederick Beneke	New York doctor, stepfather of Jennifer Goldsmith
Jennifer Goldsmith	Philosophy student at Boston University
William (Billy) Eaton	A patient at a mental hospital, former Marine Corps recruit at Parris Island
Lois Grave	A patient at the hospital, friend of Billy, recent Ph.D. in philosophy, granddaughter of Fast Eddie
Sgt. Gene Allen	Billy's Marine Corps drill instructor at Parris Island
Capt. Bonner	A Marine Corps officer investigating the charges of Sgt. Allen's maltreatment of recruits
Fast Eddie	A con man, grandfather of Lois Grave
Subway Slim	Eddie's partner
Beneficent Ben	Eddie's uncle, a con man who raised Eddie

Fr. Michael Flanagan	A former Naval Intelligence officer, Jesuit priest with a Ph.D. from Harvard, special investigator for the Roman Catholic Church, cousin of Bobby Larson
Bishop Dwight Thomas	A former Head of Roman Catholic Church's Office of Special Investigation
Msgr. Pagello	The new Head of Roman Catholic Church's Office of Special Investigation

The Twenty-Second Century

Jimmy Tagarat	A devout Christian and student at the New University on Planet M 236 in the Delta System
The Professor	An android professor at the New University
Gustav Miller	A wealthy mine owner who founded an atheistic movement known as Millerism
Virg	A guide at one of Miller's Houses of Nonbelief, an infrequent auditor of the Professor's classes

The Preacher with No Name	The mysterious founder of the God-Free Movement
Harry English	The new Head of the Neurocomputer Division of the Institute of Advanced Research on the Planet Summa
Nicka Ta	The principal investigator of the Free Will Improvement Project on Summa, alien, feminist, atheist, old school friend of Harry
Gordon Blackburn	Head of the Research Division of Implants Unlimited on Radum, Summa's sister planet

Part I

Beginnings

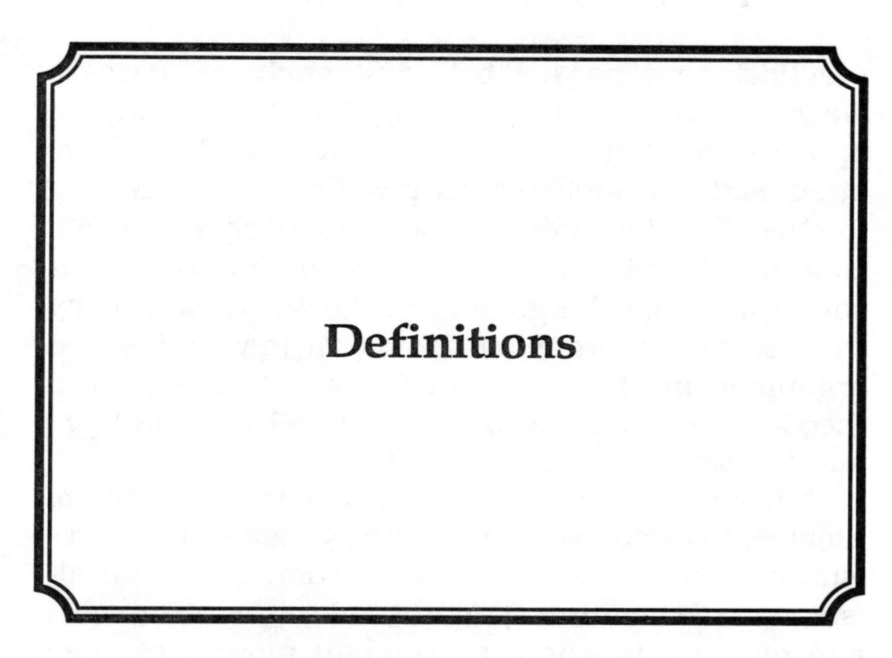

Definitions

a-the-ism: *n.* the belief that there is no God or gods. **—a-the-ist**—*n.* **a-the-is-tic, a-the-is-ti-cal** *adj.*— **a-the-is-ti-cal-ly** *adv.*

The Random House Dictionary, 1980

Atheism: (From the Greek "a" meaning "without" or "not," and "theos" meaning "god.") This could take the form of not believing in God or gods without positive disbelief (negative atheism, q.v.) or it could involve disbelief (positive atheism, q.v.). The former variety of atheism is compatible with agnosticism (q.v.). Negative atheists have attempted to establish their case by undertaking to refute traditional arguments for the existence of God—for instance, the cosmological argument (q.v.), the teleological argument (q.v.), the argument from religious experience (q.v.), the argument from miracles (q.v.)—by undermining practical reasons for believing such as Pascal's Wager (q.v.), and by showing the irrationality of appeals to faith (q.v.). Positive atheists have attempted to establish their position by endeavoring to show that the concept of God is incoherent (God: conceptual problems, q.v.), by use of analogical reasoning (analogical arguments: atheistic uses, q.v.) by the use of the argument from evil (q.v.). This last argument involves attempting to refute standard theodicies (q.v.) such as the free will defense (q.v.) and the soul-making defense (q.v.).

Atheism has been associated with a variety of nineteenth- and twentieth-century "isms" (rationalism, q.v.; skepticism, q.v.; positivism, q.v.; naturalism, q.v.; communism, q.v.; and humanism, q.v.) and movements (the Free Thought movement, q.v.; and the Ethical Cultural movement, q.v.). However, in many instances these positions and movements were not, strictly speaking, atheistic. At the end of the twentieth century approximately 20 percent of Earth's population were nonbelievers although only approximately 4 percent were positive atheists. Organized atheistic movements such as the American Atheists (q.v.) and Democratic and Secular Humanists (q.v.) had relatively few members.

In the twenty-first century atheism declined on Earth despite some attempts to revive it (such as the Down with God movement [q.v.] circa 2053) and by the end of the century only 10 percent of the Earth's population were nonbelievers. This was the combined result of the increased birth rate among religious believers and the resurgence of religious fundamentalism (q.v.).

With the experience of space exploration and colonization at the beginning of this century, human beings came into contact with a variety of alien religions (q.v.). These ranged from monotheistic religions such as Manikopoism (q.v.) and Soto Demeism (q.v.), to dualistic and polytheistic ones such as Jokalaism, (q.v.) and the Kumma W'taism (q.v.) with its thousand-and-one gods, the Kummaitos (q.v.). This contact generated increased skepticism among humans concerning their own religious doctrines, and a number of atheistic movements arose particularly on human space colonies. The most notable of these were Millerism (q.v.) on Planet M 239 in the Delta system which spread quickly to the surrounding systems and the God-Free movement (q.v.) on Epsilon III in the Argon system. This later gained a large following among the human populations of several mining planets in this system but gained only a small number of converts from the ranks of alien religions.

(M. Martin, *Atheism: A Philosophical Justification* [1990]; J. Jurgens, *The Decline of Twenty-First Century Atheism* [2096]; H. La Blanc, *Recent Religious Skepticism and Alien Religious Contact* [2142]; D. Haba, *Alien Atheism: Some Recent Trends* [2167])

The Concise Galactic Encyclopedia of Religion, 2183

The God-Free Movement (circa 2130): An atheistic movement started by an unknown preacher, sometimes known as the Preacher with No Name, on Epsilon III in the Argon system. It spread to mining planets in the system and gained a following of approximately thirty million until it was ruthlessly suppressed during the Revolt against Skepticism (q.v.) circa 2150. It is still widely followed by intellectuals, academics, and top level bureaucrats in this system although it has gained relatively few converts from alien religions. Appealing to reason, responsible belief, and freedom from belief in God, the Preacher with No Name taught the Four Doctrines of Nonbelief: God-Fall, God-Doubt, God- Rejection, and the goal of God-Free. The teachings, sayings, and legends of the Preacher with No Name have been collected in *The Book with No Name*.

(D. Haba, *Alien Atheism: Some Recent Trends* [2167]; S. Fulton, *The God-Free Movement in Historical Perspective* [2172]; J. Urwin, *The Four Doctrines of Nonbelief: An Analysis* [2160]; D. Howard, *Commentary to "The Book with No Name"* [2178])

The Concise Galactic Encyclopedia of Religion, 2183

The Preacher with No Name

The Preacher with No Name came from the western mountains and moved down through the valley preaching a creed that few wanted to hear: the Doctrine of Nonbelief. Down, down through the low country to the sea he moved, stopping in every hamlet and town until he came to the biggest cities. He spoke to small groups on street corners, to large crowds in the city squares, to passersby in parks and commons and his message was always the same. Some understood it and were frightened; some professed not to comprehend it; while others, sensing what it was, refused to hear. Yet he usually drew large crowds who at first listened in rapt attention and then, becoming anxious because of the meaning of his words, would move away out of the range of his voice.

He spoke slowly and dreamily and his words at times sounded like mystic poetry:

> Like the wind out of the west come I
> Sweep before me the dust from the sky.
> No trumpets blowing, only truth recall,
> And from Heaven and Hell God will fall.

At other times, when he spoke quickly and with great necessity, he sounded like a teacher urging his students on to greater intellectual responsibility:

> You must have the courage not to believe in things for which you have no evidence! Base your belief on the facts! Reject authority! Think for yourself! There is nothing so sad as a human being whose life is based on unsupported beliefs! If an examination of the evidence shows that there is no reason to believe in God, then you must not believe. This will be hard. You will be going against the tradition in which you were raised. You will be rebuked by your family and friends. More importantly you will have no psychological crutch! You will have no one to pray to! You will be on your own! Have courage!

Yet at still other times he sounded like a prophet who was proclaiming a new religion that offered salvation though the rejection of God:

> My friends, you have heard it said that God's commandments must guide our life and a God-centered morality must reign supreme. But I say unto you that God must become irrelevant to your moral life and that, from the point of view of morality, God must fall from Heaven! God-fall is the way! My friends, you have heard it said that doubt in God is a sin and that you must have faith. But I say unto you that doubt in God is the beginning of salvation! God-doubt is the first step!

> My friends, you have heard it said that to realize your true self you must follow God. But I say unto you that to realize your true self you must reject belief in God by disbelieving that He exists! God-rejection is the second step!
>
> My friends, you have heard it said that the goal of life is to be merged with God. But I say unto you that your goal is be free of God! God-free is the goal!

Hecklers in the crowd sometimes challenged him. Smart alecks and buffoons would shout out questions that they thought would stump him. Although he was kind and gentle when children asked questions, he was often cruel to hecklers. Sometimes he answered them in parables, sometimes with withering sarcasm, and sometimes with biting logic. Once, when he addressed a crowd by the sea, five theologians from the university came to hear him speak and pressed him to justify his views. He answered them, in what has come to be known as the "Sermon by the Sea," by showing them that their concept of God was inconsistent.

No one knew his name or his background. Although he emerged out of the western mountains, he did not speak like a westerner. His accent was not distinctive and he refused to answer questions about his personal life. He left as mysteriously as he arrived. Announcing one day that it was time for him to depart, he moved up the coast in the direction of the northern forests and was never seen again. On his last day he addressed the crowd, saying

> I have planted a seed that can grow if it is nurtured.

I have left a message that can be heard if one has ears.

Let them who are brave cultivate my seed!

Let them who have ears hear my message!

God-fall! God-doubt! God-rejection! God-free!

He gained few converts and made many enemies. Yet there are those who say that his seed is still germinating and that his message can still be heard. (From the Introduction to *The Book with No Name.*)

Letters from Lois

50 Maplewood Dr.
Westerville, OH
Dec. 3

Dear Professor Martin:

Fearful that you would reject the central argument in chapter 6, "Epistemological Problems of Autobiographical Narratives," I was greatly relieved to learn that you saw merit in my idea and propose only that I "clarify and expand the two subarguments used to support the major premise." I can accomplish this with no difficulty and have already commenced revisions. The rest of your comments on this chapter were on relatively small points that I should be able to handle with dispatch. I am completely on schedule and with luck I will be able to send you the final draft of my entire dissertation in three months.

Unfortunately, my personal situation remains the same. My mother's condition has not improved. Although her injuries are a great worry to me, so far I have managed to do several solid hours of study and research each day. While providing moral support to my father and some nursing care for my mother, I still have time to work on my dissertation and continue to do serious philosophical research at Ohio State University.

Thank you very much indeed for forwarding to me a copy of the letter that you sent to the Boston University Placement Office. Although I greatly appreciate your glowing comments, I have grave reservations as to whether I can live up to the billing. I have never considered myself "brilliant, perceptive, and hard working, with an outstanding Socratic teaching style," and find it hard to believe that my natural teaching ability is as great as that of anyone you have ever known. Be that as it may, I am deeply flattered and I am sure that your letter will aid me enormously in obtaining a teaching position.

Thanks also for sending me a preliminary draft of your forthcoming book on atheism. So far I have only read the preface and skimmed a few of the chapters. As a student of autobiography, I note with interest that you say nothing about how you became an atheist or the influences on your intellectual development in the preface. I urge you to reconsider your decision to be silent on these matters. Autobiographical remarks in the preface not only would be appropriate but could give this massive work a more personal flavor. By the way, how did you become an atheist? Were there problems in being one? Thanks again for your comments and letter.

Yours truly,
Lois Grave

* * *

Philosophy Department
Boston University
Dec. 17

Dear Lois:

I am delighted to learn of your progress on your dissertation and look forward to seeing the final draft by the beginning of February. I am distressed to hear about your personal situation but marvel at your ability to do scholarly work under these trying circumstances. Your mother's accident coming on the heels of your illness was a terrible piece of bad luck. What is the prognosis concerning your mother? Is the medicine that you are taking controlling your depression?

Yes, I agree that my preface should be revised and some autobiographical details should be provided. I am grateful to you for your honest advice. My problem is to know exactly what I should say. How did I become an atheist? Certainly, Louis Young—I always called him "Lou"—my step-grandfather, was the biggest influence. He was a self-educated man. Although he had only a fourth-grade education, he read "highbrow" nonfiction books, wrote letters that were published in the Cincinnati newspapers, and attended lectures on a wide variety of topics. All this greatly impressed my mother and father, who considered Lou to be very intellectual. Lou's influence on me was profound. As a young child I had many talks with Lou about God. He was an atheist with a definite metaphysical turn of mind and I recall vividly his saying, "It is difficult to understand how something could be uncaused; but it is also difficult to understand how a chain of causes could go on forever."

This was heady stuff for a young boy and it no doubt influenced not only my later views but even my choice of profession. Lou's influence was particularly strong since my parents had only the vaguest religious convictions, were never members of a church, and gave me no religious instruction. His influence remained with me all through my childhood in Cincinnati, my service in the Marine Corps, my brief stint at the U.S. Naval Academy, my college days in Arizona, and my years in graduate school at Harvard.

Were there problems being an atheist? Yes, but growing up as an atheist in a Catholic, lower-middle-class neighborhood in Cincinnati was not as difficult as one might suppose. When the subject of God came up in our childhood conversations and I expressed my atheistic views, they were not greeted with scorn. Whether this was the result of my friends' respect for my fighting prowess or their natural religious tolerance I do not know.

Although I was a quiet and introspective boy who kept to himself a great deal of the time, I was big and strong for my age and was considered a good fighter by my peers. Nevertheless, even as a child I was aware that my atheism was not something I should advertise. I realized that most people believed in God and suspected the worst of atheists. Indeed, I vividly recall the day in the third grade when I revealed that I was an atheist to a sympathetic guidance counselor. This confession to a stranger was such a traumatic and emotional experience that I broke out in hives a quarter of an hour later and had to be sent home.

When I joined the Marines at age seventeen, I had to declare to which religious denomination I belonged: Catholic, Protestant, Jew. Since there was no category for nonbelievers, I arbitrarily chose Protestant. Fortunately, the Marine Corps did not seem to care what one said and there was no pressure to attend church. Indeed, I never set foot inside a church until I was nineteen and, for a brief period of time, a midshipman at the U.S. Naval Academy, where I was compelled to attend chapel. Once I learned "the system" I began to peel off into the bushes as we marched to chapel on Sunday morning, and then walk back to my room and sleep. It is fortunate that I soon resigned, for eventually I would have been caught. However, I am not sure whether I should put all of this in the preface. By the way, what is your religious background? I have a feeling that whatever your past training you are not religious now. I would be interested in knowing.

Best regards,
Michael Martin

* * *

50 Maplewood Dr.
Westerville, OH
Feb. 3

Dear Professor Martin:

Under separate cover I am sending you what I trust is the final draft of my dissertation: "Philosophical Issues in Autobiography." However, I am quite prepared for any revisions that you might suggest. Although some of my fellow graduate students at Boston University will hate me for saying this, I actually enjoyed writing it. The novelty of the subject and challenge of the issues kept me from dwelling too much on my personal problems. More about these later.

Your letter of April 7 concerning Lou Young and your problems as an atheist was a great revelation. I recommend that all of these details be included in the preface. They are interesting in their own right and, as I suggested in my last letter, will set a more personal tone. Indeed, I wonder if even more background would be helpful. Readers will certainly want to know more about Lou Young. What was his background? How did he become an atheist? Obviously, they will want to know more about you. What other kinds of personal problems did you have? Did your atheism restrict your friends and marriage prospects? As you know from my dissertation, the problem of selection is of paramount importance in autobiography. One cannot include everything in an autobiography, and certain facts are excluded on theoretical and pragmatic grounds. Although such considerations do not play as much of a role in an autobiographical preface, they are still important.

I am sorry to report that my poor mother is worse. She is not responding well to treatment and the doctor now seems to believe that she may not live. Although her age is certainly a factor, the main problem is the head injury that she received from being thrown from the car. I love my mother deeply and we are very close. I am only beginning to envisage the future without her. No, my medicine has not entirely controlled my depression. Now that my dissertation is completed and I have more time to dwell on my problems, I am worried that my depression will increase dramatically. I hope I am mistaken. Perhaps in order to keep my mind occupied I should write my own autobiography!

You ask about my own religious background. I too was influenced by my grandfather. His name was

Edward Shutters. However, he is not someone I talked about very much. He was a con man whose street name was Fast Eddie. Unfortunately, he swindled people out of large sums of money. My grandmother did not know about his occupation when she married him. However, she eventually found out and left him. Fast Eddie was a militant atheist and talked about the absurdity of religious belief all of the time. Indeed, he seemed to think that religious belief was the result of a con perpetrated by the churches. I really knew very little about him except that he spoke a great deal about his Uncle Ben, who had raised him. I also recall that he was lots of fun, was wonderful with children, bought me expensive presents when I was a child, and was loathed by the respectable members of our family. In fact, he was so hated by the members of my family that he was forbidden to see me after my seventh birthday. I am afraid that the only person still alive who could tell me more about him is my mother, and she is hardly in a position to do so. I hope I will be hearing from you soon.

Yours truly,
Lois Grave

P.S.: I got a call yesterday from the Chair of the Philosophy Department at Eastview State. He wants me to come out for an interview for a position in the department. I hope I can pull myself out of my depression long enough to make the trip. Of course, I would not take the job even if it were offered if my mother is still so very ill. I will have to see.

* * *

Philosophy Department
Boston University
Feb. 12

Dear Lois:

In my judgment your dissertation is ready to be defended. Professor Denton, your second reader, agrees. I have scheduled an oral exam on April 12 at 2 P.M., room 525 of the School of Theology. I assume this date is satisfactory; if not, please let me know. The dissertation is really an excellent piece of work, Lois, something of which you should be very proud. I recommend that you try to get it published.

With respect to Lou Young's background, I would gladly include more facts, but there are not many more that I know to include. In fact, when I think back, I know very little about this quiet, solitary man who had such an influence on my ideas. I know that he married my maternal grandmother rather late in life, that he lived with my parents for almost twenty years after she died, that he was a buyer for a wholesale fruit and vegetable company in Cincinnati and made good money, that he left for work around four o'clock in the morning, that he supplied our family with wonderful produce, and that his hobby was growing roses. However, I regret that I never learned more about Lou's atheism. When Lou was a young man, did he ever get the chance to hear Robert Ingersoll, the great freethinker? What books did he read? Did he believe in God at one time in his life? I will probably never know the answers to these questions, since Lou and both my parents are dead.

You ask about whether my atheism affected my own personal relations. I did have difficulty in finding a wife with compatible religious views. However, this part of my story at least had a happy ending. The details are, I think, best left out of a short preface, and I would justify this exclusion by what you refer to as pragmatic reasons. Your own background is much more interesting than mine. Fast Eddie sounds like a character out of a story by Damon Runyon, the author whose best-known stories are about New York City nightlife. You must try to find out more about Fast Eddie! Lou Young sounds so tame and uninteresting in comparison. I am deeply sorry about your mother. Your depression also concerns me greatly. Are you seeing a psychiatrist?

Best Wishes,
Michael Martin

* * *

Evanstown, IL
Oct. 28

Dear Professor Martin:

My dear mother passed away on March 2. I went into a steep decline and for a short time had to be hospitalized. Phenomenologically, the world seemed as if it was tinted in grays and dark blues. The most trivial things would cause me to weep, and I was haunted by a ghastly vision of my mother in her last days. Desperately wanting to escape this life, suicide seemed an appealing and easy solution. As you know, this was not my first time as a patient in a mental hospital. Providing a secure and warm atmosphere, mental hospitals seem pleasant enough places to be. But for the depressive, knowing why you are there often has the effect of making you more depressed. Although very depressed, I was able to be useful in the hospital. I befriended many of the patients and taught them to see their problems more clearly. Perhaps in a different incarnation I would have been a psychotherapist.

One patient in particular would have been interesting to you. He heard voices, including God's, and believed that God was going to let him run the world for a day. He had marvelous plans for improving things. Interestingly enough, confronting him with the problem of evil convinced him that he was not hearing God's voice. Fortunately, a new drug finally seemed to snap me back to a relatively normal state and since June I have been free of deep, incapacitating depression.

The other good news is that I have taken a position at Eastview State College as an assistant professor. I have taught there now for over a month and love it. I still don't know whether you are correct about about my wondrous teaching ability, but everyone seems to think I am doing a fine job. Although I am rather excited, I am quite anxious that my depression might recur. Perhaps with the new drug and force of will I will be able to get through the academic year. In order to keep busy, last summer I explored the possibility of writing a book on unknown eighteenth-century women philosophers.

One woman in whom you may be interested has surfaced in my research. Her name is Mary Taylor, and she was an atheist and tough-minded religious critic as well as a feminist. According to her recently discovered diary she refuted Paley's Argument from Design—not in writing, but during a private conversation with Paley. I will tell you more later. At present I am writing fictional stories about Mary Taylor's meeting with Paley as a possibly fruitful way of generating hypotheses about the historical encounter.

I really have not expressed my deep gratitude for your help in completing my dissertation and getting the job at Eastview. I appreciate your help more than you can know.

Yours truly,
Lois Grave

* * *

Westerville, OH
April 21

Dear Professor Martin:

My daughter Lois took her own life on April 12. Although I suspected that something like this might happen someday, I was still not prepared for it. She seemed to be getting along very well until the anniversary of her mother's death on March 2. She was hospitalized with a deep depression and, although supervised closely at the hospital, managed to kill herself by hanging. She left you a note which I have enclosed.

Sincerely,
Clarence Grave

* * *

Langley Hospital
April 12
Columbus, OH

Dear Professor Martin:

As an infinitely heavy weight and bottomless gloom descends on my psyche, I am forcing myself to write you a few lines. My life has become dark, drab, and dismal. It is clear that I cannot go on this way and I wish profoundly that my life could end. However, I am not sure I have the courage to act decisively. Of course, I wish I could rise above my depression and I had hoped that philosophy could help me do this. But I read philosophers like Albert Camus with little profit. He maintained that the absurdity of human existence is a function of two things: the expectations of human beings and the reality that they find. Human beings expect to live in a world that is rational and unified. What they find is a world which is neither. This tension between expectation and reality generates the absurdity of existence. For many people this absurdity is too much to bear; some try to escape by physical suicide and some commit what Camus calls philosophical suicide, in which, by a leap of religious faith, one assumes, despite the evidence, that the universe is rational and unified. Camus argues that such escapes are dishonest and unauthentic. One must live one's life with the full realization that human existence is absurd in defiance of the universe to which one is unreconciled.

But my problem is not Camus's; I don't think the universe is absurd in Camus's sense. Since I don't expect the universe to be rational and unified, his theory can hardly apply to me. I agree with Camus, of course, that it is a mistake to make a religious leap of faith but for quite different reasons than he gave. Making a leap of faith to God would not be advisable for a simple practical reason: I would still be depressed even if I believed in God. In my depression I would hate life even if I thought God existed.

Thomas Nagel's theory has been of no help either. Arguing that a philosophical sense of absurdity comes from the "collision between the seriousness with which we take our lives and the perpetual possibility of regarding everything about which we are serious as arbitrary, or open to doubt," Nagel maintains that although as human beings we take our lives seriously, it is possible to take another vantage point outside of ourselves. Unlike animal and inanimate things, we can transcend our own limited perspective and see our lives *sub specie aeternitatis*. From this perspective, Nagel says, all we do appears to be arbitrary. Nagel argues that it is futile to try to escape this position by taking some wider perspective that may give our lives meaning. If we can step back from the purposes of individual life and doubt their point, it is possible to step back from the kingdom and glory of God and doubt its point as well.

However, Nagel, unlike Camus, does not recommend a heroic defiance of the universe in the face of this absurdity. This sort of dramatic response, Nagel says, fails to appreciate the "cosmic unimportance of the situation": "If *sub species aeternitatis* there is no reason to believe that anything matters, then that does not matter either, and we can approach our absurd lives with irony instead of heroism or despair."

But if nothing matters, then suicide does not matter either. Suicide is as arbitrary as everything else. Nagel's ideas can hardly provide me a good reason for staying alive. Ultimately, the decision is an irrational one, not one that can be justified by reasons and arguments.

It is likely that this will be the last correspondence you will get from me. I hope you will remember me fondly.

Yours truly,
Lois Grave

* * *

Philosophy Department
Boston University
April 18

Dear Mr. Grave:

The death of your daughter was a deep shock to me and to all who knew her. She had one of the best philosophical minds of any young philosopher I have ever met. Apparently, even in her last moments and in her profound depression, she was grappling with philosophical issues that affected her decisions. Please accept my deepest sympathy.

I enclose a copy of her note for me that you sent me and my response to it. Although my response comes too late, it is what I would like to have said to her. Please notice the suggestions I make in the last paragraph of my letter. If you approve of them, I will proceed.

Sincerely,
Michael Martin

* * *

Philosophy Department
Boston University
April 18

Dear Lois:

All of your friends at Boston University will miss you deeply. However, I wish so much you could have postponed your fateful decision until after you had considered the reasons for not taking your own life that are contained in this letter. Whether they would have changed your mind I cannot be sure, but at least they would have provided you with the opportunity to read a critical response—something from which you always greatly benefited.

I think I can understand your decision to take your own life. But I think your arguments for doing were not completely persuasive. Consequently, the decision was unjustified. As nonbelievers we both realized that life can have value, meaning, and importance without God. But because of your depression you thought life had none of these attributes. You assumed that in order to go on living you would have had to believe that it did. I think there are three reasons for believing that your thinking was faulty. First, the world, you said, had become dark, drab, and dismal. This was not, strictly speaking, correct. The world *seemed* this way to you because of your depression. The world in itself was no different than it had been before your depression. Outside of this metaphysical point, there is a pragmatic reason for not taking your own life. Depressions are transitory. Given a new medication or new therapy, the world might have seemed rosy and bright and your reason for suicide would have vanished. Finally, there is a moral reason. You had great talent and now it will never be fulfilled. Like Kant, I believe that one has a duty to fulfill one's talents. Whether such a reason outweighs eliminating the pain of your depression I don't know. But it might have.

With your father's permission I will endeavor to help preserve your memory in two ways. Your dissertation should be published. Eastview State Press has already expressed some interest. In addition, I have asked the Director of Graduate Studies here at Boston University to create an award that would be given each year to the best teaching assistant in the philosophy graduate program. It would be named after you: The Lois Grave Graduate Student Teaching Award.

Yes, Lois, we will remember you fondly.

With all best wishes,
Michael Martin

Are You an Atheist and Don't Know It?

This lecture by Gustav Miller was delivered holographically to the Intragalactic Society of Agnostics in 2121. An expanded and revised version appears as chapter 13 in Miller's book Why I Don't Believe, *published in 2123.*

It is indeed a great honor this evening for me to address The Intragalactic Society of Agnostics at this centennial celebration of the birthday of its founder, Dr. Jason Harwick. Dr. Harwick was without doubt one of the giants of the twenty-first century. Seventy years ago last month this brilliant scientist, religious critic, pioneer in space robotics, humanitarian, and distinguished poet convened the first meeting of this Society on Planet 516 in the Delphi system. He would be pleased that it has grown and prospered. Unfortunately, he did not live to see his dream of a truly intragalactic society of agnostics come true; his untimely death only two years after the Society's founding prevented him from experiencing its phenomenal growth. Starting from a modest beginning of only thirty-seven members, it has matured into a large and powerful organization of 1.5 million with over five hundred chapters throughout this part of the galaxy. However, whether Dr. Harwick would have been pleased that yours truly, Gustav Miller, was chosen to give an address in his honor is another issue.

As you know, Dr. Harwick did not consider himself an atheist. Indeed, he had hard things to say about atheists. According to Harwick, atheists are a dogmatic lot daring to claim certainty when none exists. This alleged dogmatism was anathema to Harwick, who prided himself on his free skeptical mind. He tended to put atheists only one short step above dogmatic theists and seemed at times to tolerate them only because he believed that with patience they might be made to see the light. Indeed, as his memoirs indicate, he seemed just as proud to have converted an atheist to agnosticism as to have converted a theist.

Given this background, it is with some trepidation that I pose the topic of my talk tonight in the form of the question: "Are You an Atheist and Don't Know It?" My answer is that you might well be. What implications my thesis has for this Society I will touch on at the end of my talk.

If you look up "atheism" in a dictionary, you will probably find it defined as the belief that there is no God. Let us call this positive atheism. So in this respect Harwick was correct to make a sharp separation between positive atheism and agnosticism.

Certainly many people understand "atheism" in this way. Yet many atheists do not, and this is not what the term means if one considers it from the point of view of its Greek roots. In Greek "a" means "without" or "not," and "theos" means "god." From this standpoint, an atheist is simply someone without a belief in God; he or she need not be someone who believes that God does not exist. According to its Greek roots, then, atheism is a negative view, one characterized by the absence of belief in God. So in this sense Harwick and the members of the audience this evening are atheists!

But there is more. Well-known atheists of the past such as Baron d'Holbach, Richard Carlile, Charles Southwell, Charles Bradlaugh, and Annie Besant either assumed or explicitly characterized "atheism" in the negative sense of absence of belief in God. In the twentieth century George H. Smith in *Atheism: The Case against God** maintained that "An atheist is not primarily a person who believes that god does not exist; rather he does not believe in the existence of god." Antony Flew, in "The Presumption of Atheism," understood an atheist as someone who is not a theist; Gordon Stein in *An Anthology of Atheism and Rationalism*† said that an atheist "is a person without a belief in God." A pamphlet entitled "American Atheists: An Introduction" said that an atheist "has no belief system [concerning supernatural agencies]"; another pamphlet entitled "American Atheists: A History" defined American atheism as "the philosophy of persons who are free from theism."

I could give references of a similar nature to show

*(Amherst, N.Y.: Prometheus Books, 1979).
†(Amherst, N.Y.: Prometheus Books, 1984).

that many atheists in more recent times have held a similar view about the meaning of "atheism." To avoid confusion, one should call the dictionary definition of atheism positive atheism and the type of atheism derived from the original Greek roots negative atheism. In common understanding, agnosticism is contrasted with atheism. However, this common contrast of agnosticism with atheism will hold only if one assumes that by "atheism" one means positive atheism. In the popular sense, agnosticism is compatible with negative atheism. So according to my account, members of the Intragalactic Society of Agnostics are negative atheists and this Society could just as well call itself by the title the Intragalactic Society of Negative Atheists.

Now I will argue an even more shocking thesis. (If Dr. Harwick has not already turned over in his grave, he certainly will now!) I believe that in order to be consistent, Harwick would have to embrace positive atheism. In religious matters Dr. Harwick demanded absolute certainty before he would believe or disbelieve. Thus, in his book *My Life as an Agnostic*, Dr. Harwick says,

> The position of the agnostic is clear. Since we do not know whether or not God or any supernatural being exists we must withhold our belief until such evidence is forthcoming that justifies the certainty that knowledge demands. Any other position would be dogmatic. It would assume that we had absolute assurance in matters religious.

Interestingly enough, Harwick's position is similar to the one taken by T. H. Huxley, the person who in 1869 first coined the term "agnosticism." According to Huxley,

> Agnosticism is not a creed but a method, the essence of which lies in the vigorous application of a single principle. Positively the principle may be expressed as in matters of intellect, follow your reason as far as it can carry you without other considerations. And negatively, in matters of the intellect, do not pretend the conclusions are certain that are not demonstrated or demonstrable. It is wrong for man to say he is certain of the objective truth of a proposition unless he can produce evidence which logically justifies that certainty.*

Thus, Jason Harwick and perhaps T. H. Huxley seem to be saying that no conclusion should be accepted unless it is conclusively proven. Unfortunately, Dr. Harwick was not consistent. In his scientific writings, in contrast to his writings on religion, he was quite clear that conclusions can be justified in the light of the available evidence and that this did not entail certainty. A scientist, Harwick seemed to believe, could be rationally justified in tentatively embracing a hypothesis despite the fact that the evidence for the hypothesis was not conclusive. For example, in his essay "Science and Progress," Dr. Harwick urged the tentative acceptance of Bradley's theory of hyperspace although this theory is only probable in the light of the evidence. Moreover, his own research efforts testify that he tacitly accepted the assumption that it is permissible to embrace a hypothesis that is less than certain: He tentatively accepted many hypotheses concerning space robotics although they were far from being conclusively established.

---

*Quoted in Gordon Stein, *An Anthology of Atheism and Rationalism* (Amherst, N.Y.: Prometheus Books, 1984), p. 5.

I think both Harwick and Huxley held standards that are too high with respect to religion. Positive atheists might have good reasons to believe that God does not exist without having certainty. Certainty is not demanded in science. (Indeed, as we have seen, Harwick settled for something less.) Why should it be demanded before we can make a rational claim in religion? Why should atheists have to have absolute certainty? Might not disbelief in God be rationally justified in the light of the evidence? This is indeed what positive atheists claim and I am not aware that Dr. Harwick has refuted this position. What did Dr. Harwick believe? Did he maintain that the evidence was evenly balanced for and against the existence of God? By no means! He took the problem of evil very seriously and took great delight in pointing out conceptual problems in the traditional concept of God. I don't recall that he was at all seriously persuaded by any pro-religious argument. Although I cannot find any statements in his writing in which he says explicitly that the existence of God is less probable than His nonexistence, such a view seems to be consistent with the general thrust of his position. The long and short of it is that a good case can be made that Jason Harwick was a positive atheist in everything but name. He did not recognize it because of an overly rigorous standard of justification in religious contexts that was inconsistent with his scientific writings and practice.

Let me summarize and draw some implications. In the first part of my talk I argued what is perhaps only a semantic point: The Intragalactic Society of Agnostics could just as well be called The Intragalactic Society of Negative Atheists. In the second part of my talk I argued that it is likely that your great founder was in fact a positive atheist. I do not presume to judge whether members of this Society other than Harwick are also positive atheists. But in light of my lecture, I invite you to consider carefully the question posed in the title of my talk: "Are you an atheist without knowing it?" You may be surprised at the answer. I think the major implication of my thesis is a practical one: Agnostics and atheists have more reason than ever to join forces to fight the evils of religion. It did not escape Dr. Harwick's keen intellect that despite what he saw as basic differences between atheists and agnostics they shared many goals—including the elimination of religious convictions—and should work together to achieve their ends. My thesis should make this cooperation even more feasible and appealing.

When I was asked by Lucie Barnes, the president of the Society of Intragalactic Agnostics, to speak on this august occasion, she said she wished me to give a speech that would "shake people up." I hope I have fulfilled her wish. However, I also hope that my words will bring closer together the nonbelievers of the galaxy—agnostics and atheists alike—and unite them in a common purpose. If I achieve this goal, then perhaps even Jason Harwick would forgive me for accusing him of being an atheist. Thank you and good night.

Part II

God-Fall

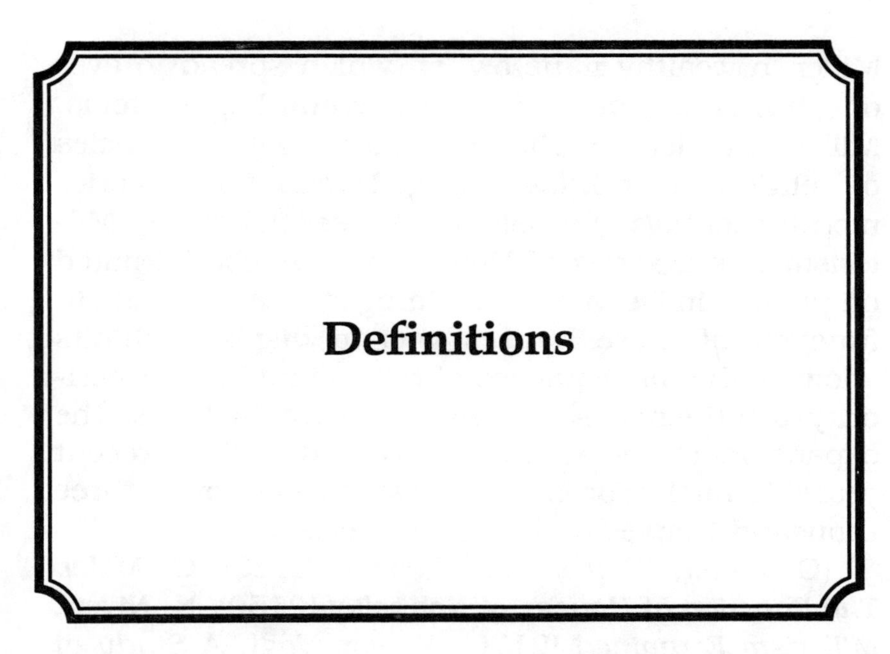

Definitions

God-Fall: One of the Four Doctrines of Nonbelief expounded by the Preacher with No Name. The term refers primarily to the rejection of God-centered morality by the God-Free movement (q.v.). Members of this movement argue that secular morality is superior to religious morality and that religion has been used to justify many immoral practices. Whether this later thesis was influenced by Millerism is not completely clear.

(S. Fulton, *The God-Free Movement in Historical Perspective* [2172]; J. Urwin, *The Four Doctrines of Nonbelief: An Analysis* [2160]; U. Goodwin, *Historical Influences on the God-Fall Doctrine* [2158])

The Concise Galactic Encyclopedia of Religion, 2183

Millerism: An atheistic movement started on Planet M 239 in the Delta system in 2120 by Gustav

Miller, a wealthy mine owner, which spread to over one hundred planets in the surrounding systems. Miller's atheism emphasized the ethical deficiencies of religious moralities and gods and the superior moral teachings of atheists. An essential part of Millerism was a series of Houses of Nonbelief situated on planets in Delta and adjoining systems. The main function of these houses was to display exhibits showing the inadequacies of religion and the superiority of atheism. After Miller's death in 2148, the expansion of the movement ceased and in recent years financial problems have caused over three thousand Houses of Nonbelief to close.

(G. Miller, *Why I Don't Believe* [2123]; G. *Miller, The Function of Houses of Nonbelief* [2150]; N. Niven, *Millerism Examined* [2170]; E. von Vogt, *A Study of the Doctrines of Gustav Miller* [2174])

The Concise Galactic Encyclopedia of Religion, 2183

An Interview with Gustav Miller

The following extracts are from an interview with Gustav Miller, the founder of the atheistic movement popularly known as Millerism and the author of Why I Don't Believe. *The interview was conducted in the summer of 2137 by Jack DeLamo as part of a Holograph Broadcasting Company's program entitled "Nonbelievers Who Have Changed History."*

JACK DELAMO: Mr. Miller, you have become one of the most popular spokespersons for atheism in this part of the galaxy. What is your basic message?

GUSTAV MILLER: Jack, if there is one thing that I would like to get across, it is that there is no reason to suppose that atheists are less moral than believers. The second thing that I have continually emphasized is the problematic nature of religious morality. Indeed, getting this second point across is the function of the lower levels of the Houses of Nonbelief.

DELAMO: By the way, how many houses have you constructed?

MILLER: Four thousand nine hundred and ninety-nine, so far. The five thousandth house will be opened next month on Elmer's Planet in the Delta System.

DELAMO: Very impressive! For those in our audience who have not visited one of Mr. Miller's Houses of Nonbelief, it is highly recommended. But be prepared to be shaken by what you experience!

MILLER: Yes, they aim to make people think and to awaken them from their dogmatic slumbers concerning atheism and morality.

DELAMO: You said that your primary goal is to convince believers that an atheist can have an upright moral character. Historically speaking, what has been the attitude of believers toward the moral character of atheists?

MILLER: In general they have thought that atheists could not be virtuous. I will give you just a few of the historical examples that I mention in my book. In 1724, Richard Bentley, an English Christian apologist, maintained: "No atheist as such can be a true friend, an affectionate relation, or a loyal subject." John Locke, who was famous for his advocacy of religious tolerance, in "A Letter Concerning Tolerance," argued, "Promises, covenants, and oaths, which are the bonds of human society, can have no effect on an atheist." Locke's belief was enshrined in legal rules that prevented atheists from testifying in court. For example, until the passage of the Evidence Amendment Act of 1869, atheists in England were considered incompetent to give evidence in a court of law. Similar legal restrictions existed in the United States. Thus in 1856 one Ira Aldrich was disqualified as a witness in an Illinois case after he testified that he did not believe in a God that "punishes people for perjury, either in this world or any other."

This is not to say that no famous believers of past centuries thought that atheists could be virtuous. Dante reserved the First Circle of Hell or Limbo for virtuous pagans. This was the abode of souls who, through no fault of their own, were debarred from Heaven. Here were found the souls of righteous individuals who lived before the coming of Christ and the souls of unbaptized infants. According to Dante, Limbo included the souls of Homer, Ovid, Horace, Democritus, Zeno, Thales, Anaxogoras, Heraclitus, Plato, and Socrates. Although Dante's scheme has many incoherences and injustices, Dante did recognize centuries ago what some theists still deny, namely, that nonbelievers can be virtuous.

DELAMO: Why do you think that atheists can have a high moral character?

MILLER: I believe that they can for the simple reason that some do.

DELAMO: Could you give us some examples?

MILLER: Certainly. I think we can all think of a relative or friend who is not a believer and yet has a high moral character. I always cite my Aunt Bessie, who was the finest and most moral person I ever knew. She was kind, gentle, always helping others. She devoted herself to her family and her community. She was truthful, courageous, and generous. Of course, few people knew about her. She was the paradigm case of the unsung moral hero. There is one small fact about her I did not mention. She was a nonbeliever all of her life!

Historically, one can cite many examples of moral nonbelievers. For instance, the eighteenth-century Scottish philosopher David Hume was described as "the Saintly Infidel." There were many virtuous nonbelievers in the twenty-first century. One thinks of Helen Davies, the first president of the Down with God movement who was known far and wide as the Secular Saint. In our century, many members of the God-Free movement have been above moral reproach and, of course, many of my own followers have a high moral character.

DELAMO: What would believers say in response to these examples?

MILLER: A theist might disagree that they are people with "high moral character." But then one must ask if the phrase "high moral character" is being used in such a way that it entails belief in God. This is surely not the way the expression is normally understood. This is not, for example, the way Dante seemed to understand it.

DELAMO: Do you go so far as to claim that most nonbelievers have a high moral character?

MILLER: By no means! It may turn out most atheists do not have a high moral character.

DELAMO: Really? Wouldn't this concern you?

MILLER: Yes, it would, but not because it would undermine my position. An atheist can admit that high moral character is a rare trait that is distributed at a low rate of frequency among theists and atheists alike. The important issue, it seems to me, is whether nonbelievers are less moral than believers, not whether most nonbelievers are moral.

DELAMO: Why do you think that atheists are no less moral than believers?

MILLER: I do not make the sweeping claim that atheists are no less moral than believers. I am more cautious than that. I am skeptical of the claim that they are less moral. I have never seen any convincing evidence that supports this claim. Indeed, I am skeptical that such evidence exists. My skepticism is based on the fact that although believers have been trying to prove their claim that atheists are morally inferior for centuries, they have failed to do so. If any credible evidence for their claim existed, believers would have found it and brought it forth. One can infer from their failure that probably there is no credible evidence.

The important point to remember is that the statement that atheists are less moral than believers is an empirical claim that must be supported by the findings of science. The fact that it seems plausible does not mean that it is true. Believers tend to forget this and think that they can know that the claim is true without any supporting evidence. Unfortunately, the empirical research is vast and difficult to interpret. Certainly some studies suggest that religion may have little to do with criminal activity, delinquency, and humanitarian behavior and that, statistically speaking, atheists are at least as well off morally as theists. However, at the present time there is no clear and definite evidence showing that more atheists than believers have a high moral character. On the other hand, there is no clear and definite evidence that refutes this claim.

DELAMO: What if credible statistical evidence was forthcoming showing that atheists tend to be less moral than believers? What would you say?

MILLER: In this hypothetical case one still could not immediately leap to the conclusion that there is a causal relation between nonbelief in God and low moral character. After all, atheists might have other traits that would causally account for the supposed differential rate of high moral character between them and theists. Their atheism might have nothing to do with their inferior moral character.

DELAMO: Mr. Miller, our time is nearly over. What about the other point that you emphasized—what you called "the problematic nature of religious morality"? Could you say a few words about this?

MILLER: I think the displays in the Houses of Nonbelief speak much more eloquently on this topic than I ever could. It may suffice for now to say that from a moral perspective religion has many problems, including hypocrisy, suppression of science, repression of healthy sexual impulses, the furtherance of war, and the advocacy of inappropriate moral models.

DELAMO: Thank you. Our time is up. You have been watching an interview with Gustav Miller. This is Jack Delamo for HBC. Good evening.

Did I Cause Smerdyakov's Suicide?

Remember Smerdyakov in Dostoyevsky's novel *The Brothers Karamazov*? He was the epileptic servant of Fyodor Pavlovitch Karamazov who advocated the view that if God does not exist, everything is permitted. Smerdyakov did not believe in God, so he murdered Fyodor Pavlovitch in cold blood. Dostoyevsky's novel attempts to show that moral anarchy is an implication of atheism. Smerdyakov's theory is commonly held. Many religious people assume that without belief in God, there would be no moral requirements and that anything would be morally permissible, including murder, rape, and theft. If Smerdyakov's theory is correct, this would be a serious problem for atheism. But is it correct? Can atheists challenge Smerdyakov's position? They can. I did.

Several years ago I wrote Smerdyakov a letter and sent it back in time to Dostoyevsky's Russia. It has always been somewhat of a mystery why Smerdyakov hanged himself. I have an idea why. I have good reason to think that he got my letter and in light of it reconsidered his position. Could he have decided that he was mistaken to believe that everything is permitted if God does not exist? Could he have realized that he had made a serious moral mistake? As a result might he have taken his own life? Here is a copy of my letter and his reply from the past. You decide!

* * *

Smerdyakov
Skotoprigonyevski, Russia
May 22, 1990

Dear Smerdyakov:

I have learned that you advocate the position that if there is no God, everything is permitted, and that you do not believe in God. I am pleased that you advocate atheism but distressed that you give atheism a bad name by defending moral anarchy. Before I indicate the problems with your view, let me distinguish the position that you seem to hold from another.

Some critics of atheism have maintained that atheists cannot have a high moral character, or that atheists tend to be less moral than believers. As we both know, this view is wrong. Even Dante believed that there were virtuous pagans. There have been atheists of high moral character—perhaps Ivan Karamazov is one of them—and there is little reason to suppose even from an examination of the evidence available in Russia that atheists are less moral than believers.

The view you advocate is not about the moral character of atheists, but about whether they can justify their actions. You claim that they cannot. Although there could be moral atheists, you say that there is no justification of their conduct. However, this view is unacceptable even to some religious believers, since it seems to be based on the Divine Command theory, which holds what is morally obligatory, forbidden, or permitted is construed in terms of what God commands or fails to command.

For example, on one version of this theory something is morally permitted, say murder, if God does not forbid it. But if God does not exist, he could not forbid murder, so it is permitted. Given this understanding, it is small wonder that you believed that you did no wrong in murdering Fyodor Pavlovitch. (Yes, I know all about this. Your secret is safe with me.)

However, there is good reason to reject the Divine Command theory. First, there is a moral problem. Presumably, this view assumes that murder is morally forbidden because God commands that people should not murder, and that kindness is morally obligatory because God commands people to be kind. In other words, God creates what is morally forbidden. If God had chosen to command murder and forbid kindness, murder would be obligatory and kindness would be forbidden. But this seems morally repugnant to many people, including many believers. Indeed, I am sure that it would be rejected by Alyosha Karamazov and Father Zossima.

There is also another problem: How can we know what God commands? How can we separate what are genuine commands of God from what are only apparent commands? This problem is serious for several reasons. First of all, there are several presumed sources of God's revelations to humans. In the Western tradition alone there are the Bible, the Koran, the Book of Mormon, the teachings of Reverend Moon and of many other less well-known religious figures. Clearly it is impossible to follow the alleged commands found in all of these books and issued by all of the people claiming to speak for God, since they conflict with one another. Furthermore, even within the same religious tradition, Christianity, for example, the same alleged command of God is sometimes interpreted in different ways. Thus, for example, the command "Thou shalt not kill!" is said by some Christians to entail pacifism and by others not to, by some to justify abolishing the death penalty and by others not to. What is the correct interpretation of the command? In addition, some apparent commands seem to many modern religious people, even those within this tradition, to be morally questionable. Thus, for example, the Old Testament forbids male homosexual relations. The New Testament forbids divorce except for unchastity. Must modern Christians follow these apparent commands although they conflict with some of their deeply held moral judgments?

Moreover, moral anarchy would not be justified in all versions of the Divine Command theory. For example, in another version of the theory—a hypothetical version—something is morally permitted, say murder, but if there were a God, He would forbid it. If God did not exist, as you and I suppose, this would not mean that murder is permitted. If we had good reason to believe that God, if He did exist, would have forbidden it, then not murdering would be morally obligatory.

So, Smerdyakov, you see that the moral theory

you assume in making your case, that if God does not exist, everything is permitted, either has serious problems, or does not lead to the conclusions that you suppose. Furthermore, there have been many secular moralities. In your own day in England, Jeremy Bentham and John Stuart Mill based their moral theories on the considerations of what brings about the greatest amount of happiness for the greatest number of people. Considerations of God and His commands do not enter into their theories at all. Other secular moralities have been based on other considerations. For example, Immanuel Kant based his moral theory on what maxims are capable of being willed to be universal laws. Again, the existence of God plays no part in Kant's justification of morality.

However, you still may wonder how there can be an objective standard of morality if there is no God. How does one confirm moral judgments? This is a difficult and complicated problem of moral philosophy that I cannot do justice to in this letter. I should call your attention to a theory that has a lot to recommend it, however. Some moral philosophers have suggested that to say that an act is morally wrong—for example, your murder of Fyodor Pavlovitch—is to say that it would be contemplated with a feeling of disapproval by a being that was fully informed, completely unbiased, dispassionate, empathetic, and consistent. I am sure you did not think of your act in these terms. You did not attempt to approximate to the qualities of such a being—a being that has been called an ideal observer. Had you done so you would have tried to take into account the various consequences of your act, including the effects on the Karamazov family and those connected with it such as Marfa, Grigory, and Grushenka. In other words, you would have attempted to be fully informed. You would have put yourself in the place of Dmitri, who was wrongly accused and made to suffer for your act, as well as of Fyodor Pavlovitch, whom you struck down. In other words, you would have attempted to become completely empathetic. I am sure that had you done this you would have contemplated your proposed murder of Fyodor Pavlovitch with a feeling of disapproval.

It is important to see, Smerdyakov, that this approach does not assume that God exists or even that an ideal observer exists. The ideal observer does not have all of the properties of God. For example, the ideal observer is not all-powerful. The theory does not say that an ideal observer does in fact exist. Rather, it states that if some act is morally wrong, then if an ideal observer existed, he or she would contemplate this act with a feeling of disapproval. Using this theory, your killing of Fyodor Pavlovitch would certainly be found to be morally forbidden. I don't want to suggest that the ideal observer theory is free from all problems, but I do insist that these problems are less serious than the problems with the Divine Command theory—the theory that you seem to assume.

So if God does not exist, it is not so clear that everything is permitted. There are plausible theories that would disagree and, moreover, the theory that does yield this result is problematic.

Yours sincerely,
Michael Martin

* * *

Professor Michael Martin
Philosophy Department
Boston University
May 30, 1851

Dear Professor Martin:

I received your letter and have studied it carefully. There is a lot to what you say. I believe now that I have been unduly influenced by Ivan Karamazov. Because of your letter, although I still do not believe in God, I am beginning to have doubts about Ivan Karamazov's teaching that if there is no God, everything is lawful. When Ivan Karamazov visited me for the third time after the murder, I told him how I murdered Fyodor Pavlovitch and gave him the money that I had stolen. No one will believe him, of course, so I will be completely safe. But I am beginning to have feelings of self-loathing that I cannot control. I regret that I did not receive your letter before I acted against Fyodor Pavlovitch.

Your obedient servant,
Smerdyakov

Miller's Inferno

Jimmy Tagarat was depressed and did not know why. He didn't like some of the courses he was taking at the New University; he especially disliked the one being taught by the android known simply as the Professor. The Professor argued in the last lecture that atheists could be just as moral as believers. This offended Jimmy's Christian sensibilities. In addition, his encounter with Virg, the strange, older student who occasionally audited the Professor's lectures, did not help. Virg had made telling points that Jimmy could not answer and this bothered him. But that was not it entirely. There was something else, something much deeper. His life and his goals all seemed without point, without meaning. It was only his Christian faith, he believed, that kept him functioning. Without Jesus as someone to look up to as a moral ideal and to believe in as his Savior, his life would be empty indeed. "Thank you, Jesus!" he often said to himself. But in his present state of mind, even Jesus seemed inadequate.

With these provocative and disturbing thoughts and feelings dominating his psyche, he walked into the woods on a dark overcast afternoon. The shadows and gloom, far from reviving his spirits, depressed them still further, and he was about to leave the woods and return to his dormitory when he saw a figure coming from the other direction. As it drew near he recognized it as the man who called himself Virg. Virg spoke first: "Jimmy! What's wrong? You look very sad."

"Does it show that much? I don't know. I wish I did. Where are you going?" asked Jimmy, noting that Virg seemed genuinely concerned over his depression.

"I work very near here—right on the edge of the woods. Perhaps you would like to come along. Things will be slow today and I can give you a private tour of some of the exhibits. Whether they will get you over your depression I don't know. Come to think of it, they might make you more depressed."

"What do you mean?" asked Jimmy.

"Well, I am a guide at the House of Nonbelief. I escort visitors, show exhibits, and things like that."

Jimmy's face lengthened. "Is that one of those places started by Miller, the mining tycoon? He's an atheist, right?"

"The answer is 'yes' to both questions. I can see that you are a little apprehensive about seeing the House. Perhaps you think the exhibits will shake your faith. Well, I have to go. It was great seeing you again, Jimmy. If you ever change your mind, let me know. And if you ever want to talk to someone, I'm a good listener. Sometimes it helps," Virg said as he started down the path.

"What do you mean it might shake my faith? I believe that my Christian faith is strong enough to withstand any exhibits that old Gus Miller might construct," countered Jimmy.

"Very well, then. Why don't you come along? It might brighten your spirits to see the folly of atheists," Virg said, but Jimmy could not tell if he was being ironic.

"All right. Lead the way!" said Jimmy, not quite as confident as his manner indicated.

As Virg had said, the House of Nonbelief was located on the edge of the woods. What surprised Jimmy was how close it was to the university and how large it was. Jimmy thought that he must have passed it many times without ever noticing it. "Seven stories," Jimmy noted.

"Actually," Virg said, "there are seven stories above ground and seven levels below ground where they keep the antireligious exhibits."

When they entered, Virg suggested that perhaps Jimmy would like to start with the Hall of Religious Hypocrisy on sublevel 1. Jimmy agreed. As they entered the hall, realistic holographic exhibits leapt into view, displaying the various hypocrisies that have plagued religion through the centuries. From the papal excesses of Roman Catholicism many centuries before to the sexual infidelities of TV evangelists in twentieth-century America and recent corruption in the hierarchy of the the Kumma W'ta religion in the Argon system, each was represented by a dramatic scene. Every exhibit was accompanied by a brief recorded lecture describing the historical context of the hypocrisies. In addition, Virg briefly commented on the exhibits, often adding biographical details concerning the hypocrites. Jimmy was greatly impressed, not only with the technical sophistication of the exhibits in the hall, which surpassed anything at the university, but with the dignity and seriousness of the modes of presentation. The exhibits induced in Jimmy a thoughtful melancholia more profound than any he had had before he entered. Although he was aware of religious hypocrisy, he had been unaware of its wide extent and severity. Nevertheless, he thought, religious hypocrisy belongs to the pathology of religion and is not of its essence.

With these comforting thoughts in mind, he let Virg guide him to sublevel 2, the Corridor of Religious Opposition to Science. As Jimmy and Virg walked down the vast corridor, holographic displays depicting scenes from the history of religious opposition to science became visible. Episodes from the history of astronomy illustrating the opposition to the view that Earth rotates around the sun, scenes from the history of biology showing antagonism to Darwin's theories, and recent incidents from the history of robotics contesting the development of intelligent androids were all displayed in vivid detail. Jimmy was somewhat perplexed by these exhibits, since the accompanying recorded lecture at each display took pains to show how religious opposition to science was based not on arbitrary decisions but on plausible interpretations of religious texts.

Although troubled, Jimmy followed Virg to sublevel 3, the Chamber of Religious Intolerance and Persecution. As they entered the chamber, they were met by holographic scenes from the Inquisition of the thirteenth and fourteenth centuries. Their realism was difficult for Jimmy to tolerate. One scene in particular became etched in his memory: A man was tied to a stake as high flames leaped around him, scorching his flesh. He screamed in agony in a language Jimmy did not understand. A small crowd of poorly dressed men and women observed him with expressions of compassion mixed with terror. Behind them stood several distinguished men in clerical robes smiling contentedly.

Jimmy's anxiety was so acute that he begged to move on to the next level. Virg led the way to sublevel 4, Battle Scenes from Religious Wars, commenting only that he thought Jimmy would have enjoyed the display of the recent suppression of nonbelievers in scenes from the twenty-second century's Revolt against Skepticism. Seeing no displays as they entered sublevel 4, Jimmy asked why. Virg explained that in order to achieve ultimate realism the battle simulator had to be used. Asking whether Jimmy had any objections to being hooked up to this device, Virg explained that the battle simulator would create a psychological experience that would make it seem that Jimmy was actually fighting a battle: He would feel the terror, pain, and anxiety of a warrior in a religious war. Virg also explained that he, Virg, would be attached to the battle simulator as well and that it would seem as if he was with Jimmy in the battle, guiding him and commenting on the passing scene.

Although somewhat apprehensive, Jimmy agreed to be attached to the simulator. *Jimmy found himself walking next to Virg down a narrow street. Partially concealed under his coat was a submachine gun. Alongside him were several other men similarly armed. As the sun began to set, the men headed toward a pub on the corner of the next street. "Where are we?" Jimmy whispered.*

"In Northern Ireland on the planet Earth in the twentieth century. You are a member of an IRA hit squad. That Protestant pub is the target. Everyone is to die. You will know what to do. Ireland forever!"

Jimmy and the other men entered the pub and opened fire. Jimmy saw a little girl running for cover. His leader pointed to her. "Get her!" he yelled. Jimmy aimed quickly and with a short burst from his machine gun shot her in the back.

The scene changed. *Armed with a mace and a lance Jimmy was mounted on a horse galloping towards a village on the edge of a sea. Virg and the other men were riding with him, similarly dressed and armed. As they neared the village the first rays of sun appeared on the horizon.*

"Where am I now?" Jimmy asked.

"You are on Earth again, this time fighting in the Crusades. Yonder village has refused to give your party a fresh supply of horses. You will now take them by force. If there is any resistance, the whole village will be destroyed. You will know what to do."

The raiding party swept into the village slashing and killing the men and women armed with pitchforks and clubs who had run from their huts. A little girl darted for cover.

"She looks like the same girl!" Jimmy thought. "How could this be?" Someone on his right said: "After her!" He drove his spurs into the horse's flank, swung his mace, and brought her down with a crushing blow to her back.

Again the scene changed. *As the sun rose above the jungle foliage, Jimmy skimmed over the surface of a lake with a hover pack strapped to his back and a laser rifle in his hands. Virg and other men similarly dressed and armed were with him. At the far end of the lake Jimmy could see a small village. He spoke to Virg over the intercom: "Where are we?"*

Virg answered, "You are at the end of the twenty-first century on Planet M 432 in the Alpha system fighting in the Kumma W'ta Insurrection. You are part of a raiding party that must secure the village. Again, no prisoners should be taken. You will know what to do."

As the raiding party reached land Jimmy cut the motor on the hover pack and hit the ground on the run. Purple-skinned aliens were fleeing from their homes and running into the jungle. Jimmy could hear his sergeant urging his men: "Waste 'em, Raiders! Waste those damn polytheists!" Jimmy set his laser rifle for maximum strength. "Tagarat! See that little purple bastard coming out of the second house to right! Get her before she makes it to the jungle!" came the voice of the sergeant loud and clear through Jimmy's earphones.

Jimmy turned, flipped on the automatic tracking mechanism, and fired. A hole the size of a saucer was burnt through her back. Jimmy thought, "She looks like the other little girls except for her purple skin and red eyes."

Jimmy sat on a chair on sublevel 4 shaking and dripping with sweat. Virg was standing over him. "Do you want to go participate in more simulated battles?" Virg asked.

"No," Jimmy replied weakly. "I think I've experienced enough of that. Virg, why did I always end up killing a little girl?"

"Why not? Innocents are often killed in war. Why should it be any different in religious wars? That you got a little girl three times in a row is purely a matter of chance. If you went through it again, the scenario might be quite different," said Virg.

As Jimmy left sublevel 4 he glanced at a large display screen listing the number of religious wars and mortality figures connected with each. He did not pause to study this chart, but he did note that the figures were high.

They descended to sublevel 5 and Jimmy asked, "What is on this level, Virg?"

"This is the Room of Sexual Guilt," Virg explained. "In order to achieve maximum realism it is recommended that the visitors be attached to the guilt simulator. It works in pretty much the same way as the battle simulator. The simulator creates psychological experiences and projects you into various historical situations connected with sexual guilt. You actually experience the guilt, agony, and psychological pain brought on by religious sexual oppression in various historical contexts. Some of the scenarios include scenes of guilt connected with masturbation, homosexuality, premarital sex . . ."

"Virg, I don't know whether I am up to this. I have already known a lot of guilt in connection with my own sexuality, and I don't think that a guilt simulator would improve things. Perhaps we could skip this," said Jimmy rather apologetically.

"Yes, of course. I was about to say, the guilt simulator is not advised in all cases, and before it is ever attached to anyone it is recommended that a battery of psychological tests be administered in order to determine possible psychological problems. If one achieves above a score of 380 or more on the Guilt Index, one should definitely not undergo guilt projection. Perhaps you would like to be tested."

"No, I don't think so. Are there any alternatives to the guilt simulator?"

"Yes, there are," said Virg. "Perhaps the easiest to

take is a holographic illustrated lecture on the history of religious sexual guilt by the Professor, who, it turns out, is an expert of the subject. It runs every hour on the hour and is about to begin. The Professor tries to make the case that religious sexual repression has been caused more pain and suffering than any other single evil connected with religion, including religious intolerance and religious wars. It is a controversial thesis which is not accepted by everyone. However, it did convince Gustav Miller, and he built it into the structure of the Houses of Unbelief. Perhaps you would like to view it now."

"No, Virg. Let's go down to the next level."

"Very well," said Virg and they proceeded to sublevel 6. As they reached their destination, Jimmy asked: "What's on this level?"

Virg replied, "Why don't I let Gustav Miller himself explain?" He pressed a button and a life-size holographic projection of Miller appeared on a small stage in front of them. A balding man in his early fifties with a kindly twinkle in his eyes, Miller spoke in a slow, measured cadence: "Welcome to sublevel 6, the Room of the Immoral Teachings of Religious Texts of the House of Unbelief that you are visiting. I am Gustav Miller. I am sorry that I cannot greet you personally; this realistic representation of me must do. In the levels above, you have seen various evils connected with religion. Some of you may think that they are easy to dismiss because they are misuses or abuses of religion and are not justified by the teaching of the religion itself. In certain cases you may be correct. But in other ones such dismissal is harder to justify, since questionable moral precepts have actually been advocated by particular religions. From the gods of ancient Greece and Jehovah of the Old Testament to the thousand and one Kummaitos of Kumma W'ta, the sacred religious books of various religions can be criticized on moral grounds. On the display panel on the wall to your right, you will see listed various sacred books that have been followed by religious believers throughout the galaxy. Simply mention the name of the sacred book you want to examine to Beatrice, your computer guide, and you will receive more information on the particular questionable morality advocated by the book. Good viewing, and so long for now." With these closing words the projection of Miller disappeared from the stage.

Jimmy and Virg stepped up to the display panel where "The Old Testament" was listed five down from the top. Jimmy said somewhat hesitatingly, "The Old Testament, please," and a soothing voice said, "Good afternoon, I am Beatrice. Your request of a list of questionable moral practices in the Old Testament has been noted. Would you prefer the subcategory of sexual practices, killing and war, diet and hygiene, personal conduct and friendship, or one that has not been mentioned?"

Thinking of his recent experience on sublevel 3 and feeling somewhat guilty that he had not pursued religious wars in more depth, Jimmy said, "Killing and war, please."

Beatrice said pleasantly, "The OT's position on killing is not completely clear. Some pacifists have argued that the OT forbids killing of all kinds. References are forthcoming." On the display screen a page from the Old Testament was displayed and "Thou shalt not kill" (Exod. 20:13) was highlighted. Beatrice continued, "But this interpretation has been challenged. The consensus of Hebrew scholars is that the sentence '*Lo Tirzach*' should be translated, 'Thou shalt do no murder.' References are forthcoming." On the display screen thirty-six references to Hebrew scholars appeared. "In addition, in many places in the OT God commands human beings to kill, and some of these commands are morally questionable. Illustrative examples are forthcoming." On the display screen two pages from the Old Testament were shown with the following passages highlighted: "Thou shalt not suffer a witch to live" (Exod. 22:18) and "He that blasphemeth the name of the Lord . . . shall surely be put to death and the congregation shall stone him." (Lev. 24:16) Then Beatrice added: "Even many religious believers have argued that these commands are ethically questionable. References are forthcoming." Hundreds of references from religious and ethical literature going back at least three centuries appeared on the display screen. She went on, "Further illustrative references of similar OT passages are available by request."

"No, that's all right, Beatrice," said Jimmy. "You can continue." "Very well," she said cheerily. "Many passages from the OT that advocate war against the enemies of Israel have a dubious moral status. Illustrative references will follow. . . ."

Jimmy had a sinking, empty feeling in the pit of his stomach. "Is there no end to this assault on what I consider sacred, no respite? No foundation that is secure from attack?" He thought, "There is still Jesus. There is still my Lord and my Savior." His heart became lighter and he said, "Virg, perhaps we should move on to the last level."

"Very well," said Virg. "That will be all for today, Beatrice."

"What is on this level?" asked Jimmy, when they at last came to the lowest level of the House of Unbelief, sublevel 7.

"This is the Alcove of Faulty Moral Models. Here are offered critiques of the teaching and ethical models of religious leaders—everyone from Confucius to Jesus to Kamsuti, the primary moral model of the Kumma W'ta."

"Jesus' ethical teachings are criticized?" Jimmy asked incredulously.

"Yes, and his ethical behavior as well. Of course, one does not have to pick Jesus," Virg said.

"Oh, that's who I want to choose. I am not interested in anyone else."

"Then be prepared for criticism," Virg said.

Jimmy felt a variety of emotions at that moment—fear, anxiety, and dread—but also excitement. How could the Son of God—a morally perfect being—be criticized? "How is it presented?" asked Jimmy.

"You have some choice in that," Virg said. "The easiest form is a straight holographic lecture by your old android friend, the Professor. The hardest for Christians to bear is to be hooked up to a simulator in which you will actually seem to experience Jesus acting in ways that are ethically suspect and propounding ethically dubious teachings. There are also scenarios in between these two extremes. I hasten to add that all of the methods of presentation are based on actual passages from the New Testament."

"Could I try an intermediate presentation? Perhaps holographic scenes from Jesus' life accompanied by some commentary by the Professor would be the best," suggested Jimmy.

"That is easily arranged," said Virg as he pressed a sequence of buttons on a panel of the wall.

On a small stage in front of them, a holographic projection of the Professor standing in front of a lectern appeared. As he spoke, he seemed to be looking directly at Jimmy: "Our first job is to try to become clear on what Jesus' teachings were. As we shall see, this is not as easy as it may seem. Once we have some idea of Jesus' ethics we must consider his gospel impartially and ask: Do Jesus' teachings provide a workable ethics? Would a sensitive moral observer agree with what he taught? We must also look beyond his explicit ethical pronouncements in two ways. We must ask: Did Jesus' actual conduct exemplify his teachings? Was Jesus an ideal moral model? Would a sensitive moral person do what Jesus did? In addition, we must ask how Christian ethicists have interpreted Jesus' sayings. In so doing we must determine how Christian ethics differs from plausible systems of secular ethics and whether Christian ethics has clear advantages over these secular systems."

Jimmy took a seat as he continued to listen.

"One initial problem is that even if one supposes that Jesus did exist, it is not exactly clear what moral principles he taught or what moral ideal his conduct was supposed to exemplify."

Jimmy turned to Virg in great surprise, whispering, "What does he mean by saying 'if one supposes that Jesus did exist'?"

Virg leaned forward and whispered, "He is alluding to a theory—it is surprisingly well supported—that the historical Jesus is a myth. An exhibit on this is found on . . ."

"Never mind," Jimmy interrupted, attending once more to the Professor.

". . . the early Christian writers said nothing about Jesus' ethical pronouncements. Even when it would have been to their advantage to do so, Paul and other early Christian writers did not refer to Jesus' teachings as stated in the Gospels. The apparent ignorance of these early Christian writers about the ethical teachings of the Gospel certainly raises serious questions about whether Jesus really did teach what the Gospels say he did. How could it be that all of them failed to invoke Jesus' views when it would have been to their advantage to do so? One obvious explanation is that the teachings are a later addition and were not part of the original Christian doctrine. If this explanation is accepted, there is no good reason to suppose that so-called Christian ethics is what Jesus taught. However, most Christians seem to ignore this problem and take the Synoptic Gospels as the basis of Christian ethics. In what follows I will adopt this convention. The primary commandment of Jesus as specified in Matthew 22:37–38 is to love God. However, this commandment had an urgency, harshness, and otherworldly quality about it that is hardly conveyed by this simple statement."

The projection of the Professor faded from the stage to be replaced by a biblical scene of Jesus surrounded by a small crowd. Jesus looked around the crowd, seemingly fixing his gaze on Jimmy: "The Kingdom of God is at hand! Sell all that you have and distribute it to the poor, and you will have treasure in Heaven; and come, follow me! Renounce everything if you want to follow me! Your family! Your mother! Your father! Your brother! Nothing—nothing I say—must stand in your way!" Pointing directly at Jimmy, Jesus said in a voice that chilled his heart, "I warn those of you who reject my teaching! You will be punished!"

The scene faded from the stage and the Professor reappeared: "In the Synoptic Gospels Jesus makes pronouncements about what should and should not be done. However, his practices yield insights into his moral character, practices that sometimes sit uneasily with his actual commandments and conflict dramatically with our idealized picture of Jesus, the Son of God and the Christian model of ethical conduct. We have been taught that Jesus is gentle, forgiving, full of compassion and universal love, offering universal salvation and redemption. Given this understanding, it is hardly surprising that part of being a Christian is believing that Jesus' life provides a model of ethical behavior to be emulated. Yet his actual behavior does not live up to the idealized picture. In fact it seems at times to contradict his own teachings."

Again the image of the Professor faded from the stage. This time it was replaced by an image of Jesus and his disciples sitting round a fire. As his deep eyes glowed like hot coals, Jesus said: "And if any one will not receive you or listen to your words, shake the dust from your feet as you leave that house or town. Truly, I say to you, it shall be more tolerable on the day of judgment for the land of Sodom and Gomorrah than for that town."

The scene changed and Jesus was talking to his disciples as they walked down a dusty road. "Go nowhere among the Gentiles and enter no town of the Samaritans, but go rather to the lost sheep of the house of Israel."

As Jimmy viewed this scene his mind was racing: "I thought Jesus was a universal Savior. What is going on?"

A woman ran up to Jesus and said, "Oh Lord, please help my daughter, for she is possessed by demons!"

Jesus looked at her, saying, "Are you a Canaanite?"

"Yes, Lord," she replied. Jesus walked away, saying only, "No, I will not help. I was sent only to the lost sheep of the house of Israel."

The woman ran after him pleading. Jesus had the woman's daughter brought forth, and he healed her.

Although Jimmy sighed in relief he thought to himself, "Without her mother's perseverance and quick wit that girl would not have been healed, although a Jewish woman's daughter would have been. Why, Jesus? Why?"

Again the scene on the stage changed. Jesus and his disciples were entering a temple in which merchants and money changers had booths. He rushed forward, turning over tables and smashing booths. Jimmy watched the money changers and merchants run from the temple in fear. "He made no effort to win over the wrongdoers by love," Jimmy thought. "Jesus taught us to turn the other cheek. This is not my gentle Jesus! Why did you do it, Jesus? Why?"

The image of the Professor returned to the stage. "In other cases, Jesus' actions were also less than compassionate and gentle. Not only did he remain silent about the inhumane treatment of animals, in one case his own treatment of them was far from gentle and kind. He expelled demons from a man, driving them into a herd of swine who thereupon rushed into the sea and drowned. I refer you to Luke 8:28–33. Clearly Jesus could have expelled the demons without causing the animals to suffer. The story of the fig tree is also hard to reconcile with Jesus' teachings and our idealized picture of him. On entering Bethany he was hungry and, seeing a fig tree in the distance, he went to it to find something to eat. But since it was not the season for figs the tree had no fruit. Jesus cursed the tree and later it was noticed by Peter that the tree had withered. Please see Mark 11:12–14, 20–21. Jesus' action not only is in conflict with his teaching that one should not use curses, but also suggests a mean-spiritedness and vindictiveness that are incompatible with his alleged moral perfection."

Jimmy's heart was beating rapidly, his mouth was dry, and he felt slightly sick to his stomach. He tried to concentrate as the Professor went on. "Jesus' practice has an additional problem. He did not exemplify important intellectual virtues. Both his words and his deeds seem to indicate that he did not value reason and learning. Basing his entire ministry on faith, he said, "Unless you turn and become like children, you will never enter the kingdom of Heaven" (Matthew 18:3). As we know, children usually uncritically believe whatever they are told. Jesus seldom gave reasons for his teachings. When he did they were usually one of two kinds: he claimed either that the kingdom of Heaven was at hand or that if you believed what he said you would be rewarded in Heaven whereas if you did not, you would be punished in Hell. No rational justification was ever given for these claims. In short, Jesus' words and actions suggest that he thought that reason and rational criticism are wrong and that faith, not only in the absence of evidence but even in opposition to the evidence, is correct. Rational people must reject an example that values blind obedience and that forsakes reason."

Feeling worse and worse, Jimmy was now having a great deal of trouble concentrating and even felt light-headed. The Professor, however, went on relentlessly. "Many Christians profess to find in the teachings of Jesus answers to all the moral questions of twenty-second-century life. Needless to say, he explicitly addressed few of the moral concerns of our own century or, indeed, of the last several centuries. For example, he said nothing directly about the morality or immorality of abortion, the death penalty, war, slavery, contraception, racial and sexual discrimination—some of the major moral problems of the twentieth century. Of the ethical status of androids and alien life forms—problems that have arisen in the last hundred years—he had nothing to say. In some cases, Jesus' silence on the morality of a practice can be interpreted only as tacit approval. For example, although slavery was common in Jesus' own world, there is no evidence that he criticized it. If Jesus had been opposed to slavery, it is likely that his earlier followers would have followed his teaching. However, Paul and other earlier Christian writers actually condoned the practice of slavery by Christians. Unfortunately, Jesus' apparent tacit approval of slavery is obscured in the Authorized and Revised Versions of the New Testament by the translation of the Greek word for slave, *doulos,* as "servant." For example, in the Revised Standard Version Jesus says that a servant is like his master (Matthew 10:25). A more accurate translation would be that a slave is like his master.

The revelation that Jesus had tacitly condoned slavery was too much for Jimmy to take. Leaping to his feet, he ran from the room. His breath coming in short gasps, he stopped in a small anteroom and leaned against the wall with his eyes closed.

"Are you all right?" asked Virg in a gentle voice.

"I will be in a short while," Jimmy said weakly.

"Of course, I am very disappointed that you could not listen to any more, since many important criticisms were yet to come. However, your reaction is perfectly understandable and not uncommon. You seemed to be particularly affected by the revelations about slavery. Why?"

"Well, I have always considered slavery one of the greatest evils in history. My distant relatives were slaves. I traced my ancestry back several centuries and it turns out that some of my remote relatives on my mother's side of the family were slaves on Earth in the eighteenth and nineteenth centuries. I imagine that they suffered horribly, and to suppose that Jesus, my moral ideal, tacitly condoned this practice is a profound shock. I am not sure what I will do," said Jimmy, looking very pale. "I think I should go home."

"Yes, I agree," said Virg. "Unfortunately, no one is allowed to leave the building without a final farewell from Gustav Miller. The message is short and will not upset you. Indeed, it might even provide some comfort."

"Very well. Let's get it over with," said Jimmy with a faint smile.

As they walked toward a door marked "Exit," a holographic projection of Gustav Miller sitting on the edge of a large desk appeared before them. "This is Gustav Miller again. Good-bye, and thanks for visiting the House of Unbelief. Some of the things you have seen and heard here today may have disturbed and upset you. If I had the power of a god, I would relegate people who commit the immoralities connected with religion that you have seen today to the different levels of Hell. But I don't. Fortunately, I do have the power to create representations of this Hell in the form of exhibits in the sublevels of this and the many other Houses of Nonbelief that are found throughout this star system. For some of you, what you have seen here today will have created a private

Hell of doubts and uncertainties about religion. My wish is only that you have been induced to reexamine your beliefs about religion and morality. If the exhibits have done this, I am content. For those of you who want to explore the positive benefits of nonbelief and learn about the great nonbelievers of the past, may I recommend that you visit the top seven stories of this building or the other Houses of Nonbelief? Good-bye for now!"

As the holograph of Miller disappeared, they boarded an elevator and rose to the ground level. The door opened onto an airy patio overlooking the woods. Virg shook Jimmy's hand. "Thanks for coming," he said. "I hope you are not too upset."

"I'll get over it. Good-bye, Virg," said Jimmy, smiling more broadly than he thought he was capable of, given his recent experience.

As Jimmy walked away, Virg called out: "If you ever want to visit the top seven stories, let me know."

"Maybe I will," said Jimmy without looking back. "Maybe I will."

Part III

God-Doubt

Howard's Prologue

Although this commentary is intended to be a scholarly study of one of the most important pieces of atheistic literature produced so far in the twenty-second century, I would be remiss if I did not point out from the outset that its central message is neither new nor unique. Although followers of the God-Free movement sometimes pretend that the Preacher with No Name's message is unparalleled, this is mistaken and misleading. The continued dissemination of this flattery among certain elements within the movement can perhaps be attributed to an unfortunate rhetorical tendency that has characterized its promulgation. The central message of the God-Free movement—that responsible belief demands rejection of belief in God—has been the essence of atheistic thought for several centuries. This is true whether one is speaking of professional atheologians or garden-variety village atheists.

This is not to deny that the God-Free movement possesses features that are not found with such prominence in atheistic movements of the past. I allude here to the strong emphasis on analysis and logical reasoning that characterized the style of the Preacher with No Name and that will be considered in detail in the body of this work. But even here uniqueness should not be claimed. Most atheists of past centuries have used arguments and analysis. Any difference between the God-Free movement and this past atheistic thought is one of degree, not of kind.

Another difference that is sometimes alleged to characterize the God-Free movement is the messianic spirit that flavors the life and teachings of the Preacher with No Name. No doubt this spirit can be found within *The Book with No Name.* However, two caveats are in order. First, this messianic spirit does not seem essential to his thought. Second, it is arguable, although by no means established with a high degree of probability, that a large portion of the messianic passages in *The Book with No Name* are the embellishments of his followers. I produce evidence for this latter point in chapter 12 of the present work.

A word should also be said about the relationship between Millerism and the God-Free movement. (The serious student of Millerism should, of course, consult E. von Vogt's classic work, *A Study of the Doctrines of Gustav Miller* [Nova Press, 2174].) Millerism might be cited as a counterexample to the aforementioned claim that the essence of atheism is that responsible belief demands rejection of belief in God and thus cited as a notable contrast to the doctrines of the God-Free movement.

Such a judgment would be unwarranted, however. Although there are important differences between the two movements that have been well pointed out by von Vogt and others, this is not one of them. Miller, no less than the Preacher with No Name, relied on the epistemic irresponsibility of religious believers to argue his case. To be sure, Miller fell back on the ethical dimensions of this irresponsibility more than does the Preacher with No Name, and in his later writing the ethical aspects were appealed to almost exclusively. But behind this appeal to ethical considerations, as his earlier writings clearly show, epistemological reasons are paramount. (See Gustav Miller, *Why I Don't Believe* [Miller Publications, 2123].)

Whether the doctrines of Miller actually influenced the Preacher with No Name is a question which scholars have and will debate. On the one hand, the fact that *The Book with No Name* contains no explicit mention of Miller and the great galactic distance between these two movements argues for the thesis held by the majority of scholars that the God-Free movement was not influenced by Millerism. On the other hand, the interesting and remarkable parallels between some of the doctrines of the two movements skillfully pointed out by U. Goodwin in *Historical Influences on the God-Fall Doctrine* (2158) suggest that Miller did influence the Preacher with No Name to some extent.

It is beyond the scope of this foreword to examine the opposite question, namely whether the Preacher with No Name influenced Miller. Again the serious students should consult von Vogt's work on this topic. The only thing that seems clear is that Miller explicitly referred to the God-Free movement only once in his writing. In an interview on the HBC in 2137, he said that the members of the God-Free movement are examples of people in the twenty-second century who are atheists and yet have high moral standards.

One final thought. Although this work is intended for serious scholars, I perhaps flatter myself to think that it may have appeal to those educated general readers of the twenty-second century who are interested in atheistic thought. The present work may indeed have such appeal if the general reader approaches it in the right spirit. Realizing that the essence of atheism is that responsible belief demands rejection of belief in God, the reader might endeavor to see the Preacher with No Name as simply a recent interesting manifestation of an atheistic spirit that has long endured and that cannot be extinguished. Indeed, the Preacher with No Name is alleged to have said something similar himself:

> My friends, my words come out of the past and will always live. My friends, my words speak to the future and will be heard again. Think not what I say is new. Think *only* what I say is true! I have come in every age and have been called by different names. But what I say remains the same! (*BWNN*, 5.46)

Douglas Howard, Prologue to
Commentary to "The Book with No Name"
(Excel Press, 2178)

Which God, Oh Lord?

Ann knelt before the starry heavens and lonely hills. "Oh Lord, I want to believe! But what should I believe? I am so confused. There are so many options, so many gods! Which God, Oh Lord? What should I do? Whom should I pray to? Are You identical with Nature as the pantheists teach? Nature is so grand and beautiful! I want to believe that You are like that! But Nature is also so ugly and cruel. How can You be identified with this ugliness and cruelty?

Are You separate from the world? Did You create the world and then leave it alone as the deists maintained? But then You are indifferent to the concerns of Your creatures—cold and impersonal—not the sort of being that one can worship and love! How can I believe in such a god?

"Do You take an active interest in the world as theists believe? Yes, You must! But then why do You seem so indifferent? Why do You let millions starve? Why did You allow the Holocaust to occur? Why do You allow . . . ?"

Ann was on her feet screaming and shaking her fist at the sky. She grew quiet and again sank to her knees.

"Oh, Lord, what should I do? Even if I believe in a theistic God, how shall I understand You? Some say You are all-good, all-knowing, all-powerful, and disembodied—outside of time and space. But, Lord, what does this mean? My poor brain has difficulty understanding. How can You have no body and yet act in the world? How can You be disembodied and be a person? On the other hand, how can You have a body? If You have a body, where is it? Are You really all-powerful? If You are, why don't You stop the suffering? But even if You are not, why don't You do things that even Your weak creatures could do to improve the world? Oh, please help me!"

Ann rose to her feet and listened. She looked to the sky and to the distant hills, but the only sound was the chirping of a distant cricket. There was no sign from the sky or the hills. Once more she sank to her knees and addressed the silence.

"Lord, what religious faith should I embrace? I was raised a Methodist. But why should I embrace this religion rather than some other Christian denomination? Why should I embrace Christianity at all? Is the choice arbitrary, Lord?"

Ann stopped her prayer and looked around. Dawn was beginning to break over the eastern hills. She felt empty and alone. She arose now and walked away. She would not come here again, she thought. Nor would she ever again address the silence. A new day was coming—a day in which gods played no role in her life and in which their silence would be no mystery. She knew that she would never again believe without good reason! She would never again sacrifice her intellect to faith! She walked through the early morning light with a new sense of confidence and hope. She would survive without belief in God! She would have the courage not to believe!

Despite what Ann had vowed, she did return there years later. But she did not address the silence of the night and she was not alone. She came on a beautiful summer day to have a picnic with her family. Surrounded by her two children and husband, her pleading to a nonexistent god in the middle of the night years before seemed strange and distant. Her thoughts were on the problems of this world, the joys of family life, and her writing. For one brief instant she tried to summon up the old emotions, but she was unsuccessful. Yet Ann remembered one part of her prayer: "Which God, Oh Lord?" Smiling, she now answered, "None!"

The Sermon on the Hill

His eyes glowing with controlled passion, the Preacher with No Name looked down from the slope of the hill and addressed the crowd below. "I preach the Gospel of Responsible Belief," he proclaimed. "You have heard it said that you should have faith. But I say to you that you should have responsible belief—belief that is based on good reasons. Let me tell the Tale of the Absent Father.

"There once was a father who had two teenage sons. He went on a trip to a neighboring city and did not say if or when he would return. After six months' absence, the neighbors said that the father had abandoned his sons. The first son, although he had no evidence to support his belief, had faith that his father would return soon and refused to prepare for life without his father. Taking note of his father's previous irresponsible actions with respect to them, the second son believed that the neighbors might be correct and started to prepare. However, the father returned after seven months, laden with gifts. The first son pleaded with the father that he should receive the gifts since he had faith that the father would return and the second son should be punished for his lack of faith. Although often irresponsible, the father was fair-minded and rejected the first son's plea. Presenting most of the gifts to the second son, he said, 'You based your assessment of the prospect of my return and the appropriate action connected with this more firmly on good reasons than did your brother. You were right to do so. Your brother had a blind and foolish faith in my return. Although he was correct, he had no basis to suppose that he was. Although I will not punish him for his illogical belief and conduct, I will not reward him as much as I reward you. You shall have most of the gifts.' "

Lowering his voice, the Preacher with No Name took a few steps down the hill. "My friends, in actual life there is seldom a fair-minded person like the father in my story that rewards responsible belief. People are usually rewarded for responsible belief by the natural course of events. People with such belief are better able to survive than those without it. For example, if the father had not returned, as seemed quite likely, the second son would have been rewarded by being prepared for the hardships of life without the father, while the first son would have been punished by being ill-prepared for these hardships."

The Preacher with No Name stopped speaking and took a drink of water because the day was hot and dry. He looked around the crowd and began again. "Oh, my friends, unfortunately theism teaches a different lesson! Unlike the father in my parable, God the Father is supposed to reward those who have faith in Him despite the evidence by giving them eternal life in Heaven, while those who have responsible belief and doubt that God exists are punished by being subjected to Hell's fire. How can God the Father be fair and still do this? He rewards irresponsible belief! The illogical faith of the first son is nothing compared to that of the believer! The religious person is told to continue to believe in a good and all-powerful God despite centuries of natural disasters that have caused untold suffering and death! The Christian is instructed to keep the faith in Jesus' Second Coming despite thousands of failed predictions of Jesus' return, including one made by Jesus himself. Jesus predicted he would return in the generation of his listeners. Mark 9:1, Matthew 16:28, and Luke 21:32 all report this.

"The first son's blind faith in his father's return after six months' absence is insignificant in comparison to that of Christians; they have been asked to have blind faith in Christ's return for over twenty-one hundred years! My friends! I say to you: Have responsible beliefs—beliefs based on reasons! But what kinds of reasons do I advocate? Let me tell you the Tale of the Worried Mother.

"Once there was a mother whose son became a prisoner of war. She wondered if she should worry about whether her son was safe. She went to her two uncles to seek their advice. One uncle said that since there was neither evidence—epistemological reasons—to suppose the son was safe nor evidence to suppose that he was in danger, the mother should base her belief on what was salutary for her. Since she would be happy thinking her son was safe, this is what she should believe. The second uncle maintained that, given the lack of evidence, the mother should suspend her belief until more evidence was forthcoming. According to this uncle, unless there are very special circumstances, epistemological reasons should prevail.

Unfortunately, the mother followed the first uncle's advice. Since there are countless statements for which there is no evidence for either their truth or falsehood, the first uncle's advice licensed belief in any and all of these things in terms of what would be salutary for the mother. For example, since there is no evidence for the truth or falsehood of the statement 'Caesar ate breakfast before he crossed the Rubicon,' the mother believed this statement because it made her happy to believe that Caesar was not hungry. The more she believed statements in terms of beneficial reasons where there was *no* evidence for or against them, the more she was tempted to believe statements when there *was* evidence against them. Indeed, it came pass that new evidence indicated that her son was gravely ill. However, since she was now so much in the habit of believing statements in terms of what was salutary, the mother rejected this evidence and continued to believe her son was healthy. As a result, she so deluded herself that she had a mental breakdown when she had to face her son's dead body after it was returned at the end of the war. The first uncle's advice was wrong!

"Forsake beneficial reasons except in very special circumstances, my friends!" said the Preacher with No Name. "Don't be like the mother in my story! If the evidence of some religious doctrine is evenly balanced there is strong presumption that you should withhold your belief until more evidence is forthcoming. But are there no special cases where beneficial reasons should prevail? Let me tell you the Tale of the Mad Bomber.

"Suppose a nonbeliever is kidnapped by a religious fanatic with access to bombs, who will kill him and blow up ten major cities on his planet unless he believes in God. Suppose the nonbeliever has good reason to believe that if he undergoes two months of rigorous religious indoctrination, he will accept God. To make the case crystal clear, let us suppose that very few people will know of his conversion, that the fanatic will die in three months, that the fanatic has no disciples to carry on his work, and that the effects of this indoctrination will disappear in four months. Presumably, in such a case there would be good grounds for undergoing the religious indoctrination. Even the most militant nonbeliever would perhaps admit that in this circumstance, refusing to convert would serve no purpose; indeed, it would be an act of insanity. Here would be a clear case where beneficial reasons should prevail.

"However, my friends, make no mistake! The use of beneficial reasons in special circumstances must be scrutinized carefully for both the likely benefits that will result from belief in terms of beneficial reasons and the possible long-term adverse effects on society, its institutions, human personality, and character. Use beneficial reasons to justify belief sparingly and judiciously, my friends! Such is the path to God-Doubt and ultimately the goal of God-Free!"

During his sermon the crowd seemed at times to be held in rapt attention by the wisdom of his words and energy of his delivery, but at other times it seemed restless and uneasy. Now he was finished and he smiled down at his audience. He descended from the hill and walked among them, offering words of encouragement and comfort. He wondered whether they really understood him and if they did, whether they would be able to follow his advice. He was not sure. He felt as if his ideas had touched few souls and had little effect. As the crowd dispersed he forlornly slung on his backpack and headed for the next town. Yet some in his audience later proclaimed that many in the crowd did understand him and were moved to God-Doubt. (From *The Book with No Name.*)

The Big Domino in the Sky

As I walked slowly down the hall to the classroom, I was deep in thought about the topic of today's lecture: The Cosmological Argument, the argument from First Cause for the existence of God. I loved to present this argument to beginning philosophy students, since it had been my introduction to philosophical argumentation in discussions with my grandfather. My thoughts leaped back to my boyhood in Cincinnati and my conversations with Lou.

* * *

As usual, Lou was out in the backyard when I arrived home from school. I made myself a peanut butter sandwich while through the kitchen window I watched him digging around a rose bush. I wanted to talk to him, but I knew better than to interrupt.

When would he ever finish? Finally he put down his rusty shovel and came into the house. Sitting in his old arm chair in his bare feet, with one leg tucked under him, he looked proudly out the window at his roses. "Lou," I asked, "remember the stuff about causes that we talked about?"

"Sure," he said. "Did you have any other ideas about it?"

"Well, Dick Minche and I got in a big argument yesterday at school."

"About what?" Lou asked.

"He said that God exists because there's got to be a cause of everything."

"You mean he thought that God exists because everything has a cause and causes can't go on forever and the first cause is God?"

"Yeah."

"What did you say?"

* * *

As I finished the presentation of the Cosmological Argument to the class, I was aware that in the back of the room Peter Evans, the wise-guy transfer student from Cornell, was talking to a red-haired young man he always sat near. "That's the argument. Although it has many variations, the basic idea is that in everyday life we discover that things are caused by other things. But an infinite series of causes is impossible. So there must be a first cause, and this first cause is God. The crucial question is whether this argument is sound. Do you remember what a sound argument is? It is an argument in which the premises are true and the conclusion follows from the premises. So this argument might go wrong in two ways. The premises might be unsupported by the evidence or the conclusion might not follow. Do any of you think that the Cosmological Argument has either of these two problems?"

No one raised a hand, although in the first row Jennifer Goldsmith, the small, dark, young woman who had received the highest grade on the midterm exam but had never said a word in class, had a knowing look on her face.

"What about the second premise of the argument? Does anyone have doubts about the impossibility of a infinite series of causes?" I said, lowering my voice slightly. I noticed as I spoke that Peter Evans was still whispering to the red-headed young man and that Jennifer Goldsmith's eyes were open even wider than usual.

"Let me clarify the problem with an analogy. Imagine a row of falling dominos. According to the argument this row of falling dominos must have a beginning. There could not be an infinite series of falling dominos, one that goes on back, back forever. There must have been a first domino that was not itself caused to fall by some other domino. Does anyone think that there could be an infinite series of falling dominos?"

Jennifer did not raise her hand but her expression indicated in the clearest possible way that she wanted to say something. "Jennifer, what do think?" I asked.

She looked shocked and yet pleased that I had called on her. "Well," she said, her voice surprisingly strong and confident, "I don't see why there couldn't be. There are infinite series of numbers in mathematics. Why couldn't there be an infinite series of falling dominos?"

"That's a lot of dominos!" said Peter Evans, and several students laughed loudly.

* * *

"Well, I said that maybe causes could go on forever and why did he think they couldn't."

"That was the right thing to say," Lou said gently. "What did Dick say to that?"

"He just laughed and said that what I said was dumb. He said everyone knows causes can't go on forever."

"Did you reply?"

"I felt like belting him one but I didn't. I said that just because everyone says that causes can't go on forever doesn't mean they can't."

"What else happened?" he asked, smiling.

"Well, I had another idea, but I didn't say anything to Dick about it. I wanted to talk to you first."

"What's that?"

* * *

Peter Evans looked very pleased with himself. He leaned back in his seat, smiling and casting glances at the person sitting next to him. "Very funny, Pete," I said after the laughter had died down. "However, I hope you don't think you said anything to refute Jennifer's point." Peter's smile faded. "Might there be another problem with this argument? What's the conclusion of the argument?" I asked.

Surprisingly, the hand of Bill O'Connor, the two-hundred-sixty-pound football player, shot up. "Yes," I said, pointing to Bill. "That God exists!" he shouted.

"Right! Does this conclusion really follow? Even if

there couldn't be an infinite series of causes and there has to be First Cause, does the first cause have to be God, an all-powerful, all-knowing, and all-good being?"

* * *

"Well," I added with hesitation, "Why does the first cause have to be God? It could be somethin' else."

"What else?" he asked.

"I don't know. That's what I wanted to talk to you about."

"Okay. Is God supposed to be good?"

"Sure! He's supposed to be . . . I get it! You mean the first cause might not be good!" I said, almost shouting.

"Why not?" Lou asked.

* * *

Peter Evans in the back of the room was looking glum. I knew he was bright despite his tendency to play the buffoon. Could he possibly redeem himself? "Peter," I said, "suppose there had to be a first domino—in other words that the series of falling dominos could not go on forever. What kind of domino would the first domino be?"

Peter thought for some time. "I guess the only thing it would really have to be is a domino that caused itself to fall. That kind of domino would start the whole series falling."

"And the application of this to the Cosmological Argument, Peter?" I asked, hoping that he would come through.

"The only thing that argument might prove is that there is a first cause but not necessarily God?"

"Outstanding!" I said. Peter beamed. I was about to go on when I saw Peter waving his hand with a look on his face that I knew all too well. Perhaps I should not have allowed him to redeem himself. "Yes, Peter?"

"Well, maybe the argument proves not that God exists, but that there is Big Domino in the Sky that started everything!" I had to resign myself to the loud snickering that would follow his comment.

* * *

Lou went on: "Is God supposed to be all powerful? Conscious?"

"Sure! You mean the first cause might be neither all powerful nor conscious?"

"What do you think?"

* * *

Now Jennifer actually had her hand up. "Yes?"

"Well," she said, "I wondered about something else. The premise of the argument is that an infinite series of causes is impossible.

"Yes, go on," I said, sensing then that Jennifer had found her stride.

"There are all kinds of different series of causes."

"And?"

"All of these different series would have a first cause."

"And?"

"There could be different first causes for the different series!" she said breathlessly.

"You mean that even if we grant the premise about there not being an infinite series of causes, the argument does not prove there is *one* First Cause?"

"Yes!" she said with delight. Even Peter Evans looked impressed, and big Bill O'Connor gave a soft, appreciative whistle.

* * *

"Thanks, Lou!" I said. "I guess I'll go out and play now. I sure will have some things to say to Dick Minche when I see him." Lou smiled and gazed out the window again at his beloved roses.

Mary and the Creators

The following story by the late Lois Grave was found among her papers after her suicide and was first published by Eastview State Press in a collection entitled Philosophical Essays and Stories. *It is reprinted here by permission of the Eastview State Press and her father, Clarence Grave. In a letter to her teacher, Michael Martin, she indicated that she saw this and other stories about Mary Taylor as a possibly fruitful way of generating hypotheses about the actual historical encounter between Paley and Taylor. Margin notes indicate that Grave used the Creators of her story simply as a dramatic way of making a philosophical point and did not intend them to indicate her belief in finite supernatural beings.*

They came out of the infinite chaos creating new worlds without end. When they were moderately satisfied with their results, they moved on to other metaphysical plains and ontological dimensions. Ere they were content, many worlds were botched and abandoned, many universes destroyed and rebuilt. They would sometimes look down on their creations and say, "This is good but not good enough!" They would just as often gaze on their handiwork exclaiming, "This is bad!" or "We can do better!" Thus, the Creators were driven by a restless surging of creative power that made them never completely satisfied with their products.

How the Creators themselves came into being even they did not know. Some of them guessed that they had been created by an earlier race of Creators, who were in turn created by a still earlier race of Creators, and so on, forever. Others believed that their race had always existed and, thus, that they were coeternal with the universe itself.

The Creators had vast but finite power and were certainly not completely good. Indeed, driven by their enormous creative energy, they were often proud, ambitious, and ruthless. Their creatures' happiness did not matter to them: the glory, beauty, and novelty of their creations did. Although they had immense knowledge, they were not all-knowing. They often miscalculated the consequences of what they had fashioned and did not understand completely the swirling chaos from which they drew their raw materials. Working together, they managed to combine their knowledge in constructing new worlds. When they cooperated, their combined power was glorious and awesome. There were many millennia in which they erected trillions of nebula, governed by elegantly simple natural law, populated by creatures of amazing intelligence and moral integrity, all enclosed in a space-time continuum of complex and manifold dimensions. At these moments the Creators relished and savored their work and strove to surpass themselves.

But billions and billions of years also passed in which the Creators were despondent over their creations. During these times they made untold universes that disappointed them and made them ashamed. Sometimes their work so revolted them that they did not even destroy it. "Let us preserve this universe" they would say, "as a reminder of what we should not do. From time to time use it as a model of world creation gone wrong." So saying, they would leave this created world, returning eons later to survey their blunder.

In a star system in one galaxy in one universe there is a planet called Earth, the only planet in the system inhabited by intelligent life. This intelligent life sometimes discussed the origin of the world in which they lived. One popular theory proposed by the intelligent life was that the universe was created by a being called God. The intelligent life developed various arguments to prove the existence of this being. One such argument was called the Argument from Design—the Teleological Argument.

* * *

"The Archdeacon of Carlisle, Reverend Paley, is giving the sermon today," said Mrs. Taylor to her daughter, Mary. Mary nodded. She was looking forward to hearing the great man. She knew that Paley was the author of several learned treatises defending Christianity as well as an impressive speaker. Indeed, she had tried to borrow one of his books on theology from her cousin, Robert, a student at Cambridge. However, her father had found out and forbidden it.

"I will not have a daughter of mine filling her head with a lot of logic-chopping, theological arguments," he had roared. "Mary needs to find a husband, not to refute some obscure theologian."

Mary loved to refute the arguments of theologians and anyone else who had the audacity to put forth arguments. "She thinks like a logician," her father used to complain. "How can she ever expect to get a husband when she finds the fallacies in her suitors' proposals?"

"Reverend Paley is not obscure, father," Mary said gently as they drove to church. "Indeed, he is one of the best known theologians in England. His treatise on . . ."

"Please, don't contradict me," said Mr. Taylor, trying to be patient. "Whether he is obscure or not, his writing is not meant for feminine consumption. Indeed, I have serious reservations about your hearing him. After the sermon I would thank you to keep your comments to yourself. Many a good lesson has been spoiled by your probing questions on the way back from church."

"Yes, Father," said Mary.

In her pew Mary sat in rapt attention as Reverend Paley argued in general terms that the intricate workings of nature and of organisms, the complex interrelations of parts and wholes, the subtle connections among aspects of the world, could be used as evidence to support the hypothesis that the universe was fashioned by some Great Intelligence. An argument for the Deity, he said, should be based on analogy. Since the universe is analogous to some human artifact which one knows is designed, the universe itself is probably designed. Paley then started to lecture on the watch analogy that Mary had heard about from her cousin Robert. Reverend Paley maintained that just as we can infer that a watch found on a heath has a designer, so we can infer that the universe has a designer. His words rang out to the assembled congregation: "Every indication of contrivance, every manifestation of design which existed in the watch exists in the work of nature; with the difference, on the side of nature, of being greater and more, and that in a degree which exceeds all computation."

As she filed out of church, Mary's mind was active. The watch analogy, which was crucial to the Reverend Paley's case, was very troublesome. She thought, "If the analogy of the watch were carried to its logical extreme, one would end up with conclusions not acceptable to the Archdeacon or any other good Christian, including Mother and Father. Watches are usually made by many intelligent beings. Thus, the argument implies some form of polytheism rather than monotheism! Also, the beings who create a watch have bodies, so God must have a body. But this is absurd! If a watch has imperfections, we have grounds for supposing that the watchmaker is not perfect. So, since the the universe has imperfections, one should conclude that God is not perfect. But this conflicts with Christian doctrine."

As Mary got into the carriage, she thought of still another point. "Are not other analogies possible? The universe is like a plant in certain respects and like an animal in others. If we follow through on these analogies, we arrive at rather different conclusions than the one favored by the Archdeacon that the universe was created by Divine Intelligence." Mary's thoughts were interrupted her father's voice. "In my opinion, a splendid and edifying sermon," said Mr. Taylor.

Mary remained silent and cast her eyes toward the floor. Mr. Taylor looked at his brilliant daughter for a long time. Finally he said, "I infer from you demeanor, Mary, that you found no fault with today's sermon."

"Well," said Mary, brightening, "there were one or two small points that . . ."

Mrs. Taylor put her hand on her daughter's arm and Mary stopped. "Yes, Father, the sermon was quite splendid."

* * *

Returning after countless eons, the Creators surveyed what they believed to be one of their blunders. They focused on a star system in the galaxy where there is a planet called Earth, the only planet in the system inhabited by intelligent life. "Notice the third planet in this system," said the First Creator.

"The intelligent creatures who inhabit it are pitiful and rather stupid," remarked the Second Creator.

"Yes, and their effectiveness is severely hampered by the many diseases and natural disasters that afflict them," said the Third Creator.

"We could have done much better," said the Fourth Creator.

"What a shame!" said the Fifth Creator.

"Should we destroy it?" the First Creator asked.

"By no means," replied the Third Creator. "We can learn from our mistakes."

"Notice how they cannot even infer from the facts," said the Fifth Creator.

"The creature called Paley is a prime example," remarked the Second Creator. "He infers that his world was created by God, an all-powerful, all-good, all-knowing being!"

"Yes, yes, it is quite absurd," said the Third Creator.

"But, I notice with interest that not all of our creatures are so dense. Note well the creature called Mary Taylor! She makes most of the correct inferences," said the Fifth Creator.

"So she does!" said the First Creator.

"But even she hesitates and is unsure of herself," noted the Third Creator.

Finally, the Sixth Creator spoke. "I do not recognize this universe."

"What do you mean?" asked the Fourth Creator.

"I do not think we created it," he replied.

"What? That is nonsense! How could it be brought into being without us?" the Fifth Creator demanded.

"Universes could arise out of nothing. They could be created spontaneously. I have suspected for many eons that this sometimes happens," the Sixth Creator said.

"A preposterous idea!" exclaimed the Second Creator. "How can you explain the order and apparent design in this universe without us?"

"Given enough time and enough spontaneous creations, surely some universes would show high degrees of order," the Sixth Creator said.

"This speculation is idle! Even if this is not one of our creations, it is surely like countless others that we did create. It can still serve a purpose and should not be destroyed despite its imperfections," said the First Creator.

"Still, the thought that worlds can arise without us is disturbing. One wonders if such spontaneously generated worlds could surpass the ones we have created," the Third Creator said.

"Enough! Let's go! We have learned all we can here for the moment," said the Second Creator. "We shall return anon!"

"New worlds await our construction!" said the First Creator.

So saying, the Creators, somewhat sobered by the new idea, disappeared into the infinite chaos to look for new opportunities to build universes and construct worlds.

* * *

As they arrived home from Church, Mary had further thoughts on Paley's sermon that she took care to keep to herself. "Could it be possible," she wondered, "that our universe came from nothing? That it just popped into existence? If enough such universes popped into existence, surely some might be like Reverend Paley's watchlike universe, that is, like ours! Should I broach the possibility with Father? No, I'd better not. I will talk to Robert when he is here for the holidays. Oh, how I wish I were a man!"

So You Wanna See God?

The Circus was in town and Harry, although nearly seventeen, was looking forward to going with almost childish anticipation. So were other members of Harry's circle of friends. Although they were the same age as Harry, none had ever seen a real circus before, and they felt deprived. This was the first space-age circus to visit Plainview, the city where Harry and his friends had lived all their lives, and, given the isolated location of the town on the mining planet, M 789, in a distant region of the Argon system, it would be the last one for a long time. Harry had talked with this friends about the circus for weeks and finally they had decided to go together on Tuesday.

When they arrived at the circus grounds, Harry was surprised at how similar they looked to those he had seen in old picture books. The Big Top, the Ferris wheel, the merry-go-round, and the side shows all looked familiar. But there were not just lions, tigers, and elephants. The wild animals were from all over the galaxy, including ferocious ten-legged zerots from Easton's planet in the Alpha 3 system, and the so-called devil cats—huge, red, feline creatures—from the jungles of an unnamed planet in an unnamed system on the fringes of the galaxy. There were also a number of genetically constructed creatures such as kongs, the huge, apelike monsters who were especially designed for doing heavy labor on mining planets. The wild animal trainer—who called himself the Great Sommelo—put this menagerie through its paces in a way that delighted children and amazed adults. There were other differences as well. For example, instead of shooting clay pigeons with BB guns for stuffed animal prizes, one shot small, birdlike robots with laser rifles for beautiful holographic pictures. Instead of human clowns who made the children laugh, there were robot clowns that the children could take home if their parents were willing to pay ten intergalactic credits. And the circus barkers called out, "Step right up and experience exotic thrills and pleasures from all over the galaxy!"

Harry and his friends had a wonderful time and were just about to go home when they heard the raucous voice of a barker. "You say you wanna see God? You say you wanna experience the ultimate? Well step right up, folks, and be attached to the Religious Experience Machine! This machine will transport you beyond time and space! You will meet your Creator face to face! You will meet your Redeemer! The experience is perfectly safe! It is recommended by the Intergalactic Council of Churches as a way of enhancing religious faith! For one tenth of one intergalactic credit you will be able to claim that you saw the Big Guy in the Sky! Don't be bashful! Don't be shy! Step right up!"

Several of Harry's group were very interested in being attached to the Religious Experience Machine. They read one of the pamphlets available in the front of the tent that assured customers that the experience was perfectly safe for everyone. They all finally agreed to go and to discuss their experiences afterwards at Glen's Place, the local high school hangout. Harry was apprehensive, but the Religious Experience Machine looked harmless enough. It was a small black box with dials on the top. Attached to the box was a wire, which in turn was attached to something that looked like a football helmet.

A young woman told Harry to sit down and make himself comfortable and then placed the football helmet-thing on his head. "To what religious denomination do you belong?" she asked. Harry looked blank. "Are you Catholic, Protestant, Jew, Buddhist, Moslem . . . ?" she asked.

"I was raised Methodist," said Harry.

"Very well," she said, smiling as she made an adjustment on a small dial. "Now, what kind of religious experience do you want?"

"Do I have a choice?"

"Yes, indeed!" she said. "There are many kinds of religious experiences. Perhaps you would like to glance at our informative brochure before you make up your mind," she said, handing Harry a glossy pamphlet.

In looking over the brochure, Harry decided that mystical experiences were not for him. They were supposed to be hard to describe and he wanted to be able to tell his friends about what he had experienced. Then there were experiences of what the brochure called ordinary objects seen in a religious way. As the brochure put it, "One can experience an ordinary nonreligious object as a supernatural being; for example, a dove as an angel." This was a little too subtle for Harry. If he saw an angel he would want to see a beautiful being with wings. No, he did not want to see a dove as an angel. So should he go for seeing an angel? Surely he could do better than that. What about Jesus? Could he have an experience of Jesus? He read more. The brochure said that the experience of a supernatural being can involve no sensations at all. "A person may experience God and not claim to have had any particular sensations." It mentioned St. Teresa, who was conscious of Jesus at her side although she did not see anything. Harry was not sure he understood this, but insofar as he did, he did not think that this was what he wanted. He wanted to see Jesus, not just be conscious of Jesus at his side.

The young woman returned to the room. "Have you made up your mind?" she asked.

"Yes, I want to see Jesus. I don't want to see him as something else. I don't want to just be conscious of him. I want to actually see him, touch him, and all that stuff."

"Yes, of course, you want the classic type A religious experience. There will be no problem with that." She turned a few dials and asked, "Are you ready? The experience will begin soon."

In a few seconds Jesus was standing before him just as Harry had always pictured him. He looked to be in his early thirties and was dressed in a plain white, flowing robe and without shoes. There was no beautiful music that filled the room, and there was no halo above his head. Indeed, Jesus looked quite ordinary except for a smile that radiated deep compassion. Harry felt deeply at peace with himself and the world. Harry moved forward in order to kiss the hem of his robe. As his lips touched the robe, it all faded. He was standing alone in the middle of the room. Jesus and the feeling of peace were gone. The young woman stepped forward and removed the helmet from his head. "I am afraid your time is up. Please exit to your left! Have a nice day!" she said.

At Glen's Place, Harry and his friends compared their experiences. They differed widely from person to person, depending on the religious tradition in which each person had been raised. For example, Abu Naser, who was raised a Sufi Moslem, said that he had a mystical experience. As the brochure predicted, he had great difficulty describing exactly what he saw, and when he tried no one could understand him. For example, he said that his experience was of motion that never moved, of light that was infinitely dark. Harry was thankful he had not chosen this type of experience. Nga Sung, who had a Buddhist background, also had difficulty describing her mystical experience. When attempting to, she lapsed into contradictory and paradoxical statements just as Abu had done. Debbie O'Brien, who said she was raised Catholic, had a vision of the Virgin Mary, who she described "as a beautiful lady dressed in a white dress with a blue sash and a yellow rose on each foot holding a yellow rosary." Haava Boma, one of the two nonhumans in Harry's class, had perhaps the most interesting experience. Raised in the religious tradition of the Kumma W'ta, a polytheistic religion that held that the world was created by strange amphibious creatures, the Kummaitos, he had an uplifting vision of thousands of Kummaitos doing a cosmic dance. Nicka Ta, the other nonhuman, on the other hand, had the least interesting experience. An avowed atheist whose family was influenced by the God-Free movement, she reported only that she experienced a feeling of harmony with nature and a sensation of love for all sentient beings.

The next day they discussed their experience with Mr. Yoon, their philosophy instructor. He raised a question that had been in the back of Harry's mind. "Do you think that the experience you had yesterday provides good evidence for the existence of what you believe in your respective religions? God? Jesus Christ? The Kummaitos?"

"Well, I do," said Debbie. "I saw the Virgin Mary just as well as I see Harry now."

"But Debbie, how do you know that what you saw was not created by your own mind? You know people take drugs and see things that are not real. The Religious Experience Machine might be like taking drugs. It creates hallucinations," said Nicka.

"Yes, but the experience I had seemed so real," Debbie replied.

"It sure did," said Harry, remembering his vision of Jesus.

"I think Nicka's point is that just because an experience seems real, that does not mean that it is," Mr. Yoon suggested. "There is a further point. Could all of your experiences be true? I mean could they really be what they are supposed to be?"

"Why not?" asked Abu. No one seemed to see why they could not be.

"Well, Harry had a vision of Jesus, and Jesus is supposed to the Son of God. Right?" said Mr. Yoon. "But Haava had a beautiful vision of the Kummaitos. Right? Now, according to Christianity, there is only one God. But, according to Kumma W'ta, how many gods are there supposed to be?"

Only Haava had her hand up. "It is written in our holy book that the Kummaitos number a thousand and one. The wise people say that this is just a way of saying that the number of Kummaitos is very large."

"Hey," said Harry, "both of us can't be correct! If my vision is true, then Haava's is not."

"That's right," said Mr. Yoon. "Harry's vision fits in with monotheism, a belief in one god, while Haava's fits in with polytheism, a belief in many gods. But monotheism and polytheism cannot both be true."

"What about my experiences?" asked Nga.

"Yes, and what about mine?" asked Abu.

"I don't see how Abu's experiences could prove much of anything," Nicka replied. "They did not make any sense! How can anything be moving and not in motion? Light and infinitely dark? What Nga said was not any clearer!"

"Well, I don't care," said Nga. "What I experienced was hard to describe. To me it meant a lot!"

"Yes, I am sure it did, Nga. But the crucial question is whether a person can take this as evidence for the beliefs of his or her religion, for example, the existence of God," Mr. Yoon replied.

"We don't believe in God anyway" said Nga. "I never said my experience was of God!"

"That's just the trouble!" said Nicka. "Your experience was like Abu's and he *did* say it was of God!"

"What about Nicka's experience? She did not experience anything religious," Harry said in a loud voice.

"Well, if your experience is evidence of God and such stuff, mine is evidence of the opposite," Nicka said, smiling.

"Yes, the reports about your various experiences do seem to cancel one another out," Mr. Yoon said softly.

"Mr. Yoon, what did people do before the Religious Experience Machine was invented?" asked Abu.

"They still had religious experiences. They fasted, meditated, prayed, and did other things to achieve them. It was harder to achieve them, of course, and many people think that the experience achieved in old ways were more genuine. In fact, some people even now refuse to use the Religious Experience Machines, claiming that the experiences they provide are artificial and unreal. But the problems are pretty much the same whether one uses the machine or achieves the experience in more natural ways. How can one tell that these experiences are not just subjective? People in different religious traditions had different experiences that supported conflicting religious beliefs. Further, some people prayed, fasted, and so on and did not achieve the experience of God or anything supernatural. Why shouldn't these negative experiences count against belief in God or whatever? Furthermore, mystical religious experiences do not make literal sense and could be interpreted as supporting different religions."

On the way home that day, Harry thought over what Mr. Yoon had said and tried to recall his experience of Jesus. The experience seemed so real! Could it really have been a hallucination? How could one reconcile the different religious experiences that they had had as well as the different religious experiences people who fasted and prayed had had? He decided that there was no way of telling whether religious experiences were real or not. In fact, Mr. Yoon had suggested that religious experiences were "an epistemological dead end." He was probably right. Harry would try to forget his Jesus experience and remember more mundane aspects of the circus. This was not hard to do. The animal act was marvelous. It was astounding how the Great Sommelo made the devil cats jump through the hoop, how he got the giant kongs to stand on their heads, and how even the zerots obeyed the flick of his electronic whip! Harry's eight-year-old nephew would love to see it. Who was he kidding? Harry would love to see it again himself. Taking his nephew would be a good excuse!

The Miracle Sleuth

Father Mike Flanagan was tired and depressed. He had just completed a long report and he was not looking forward to presenting it to Monsignor Pagello. He leaned back in his chair, stretched his muscular body, and sighed. "The Monsignor will not like it. He will not like it one damn bit. But what could I do? It's the truth," he thought. Unfortunately, he knew that the Church sometimes had to bend the truth for its own noble ends. He did not mind that. Mike was enough of a utilitarian to know that truth was not everything and that sometimes it had to be sacrificed. What he hated was the pretense: the denial that the truth was being bent for good purposes.

"Why couldn't they just admit that they were lying for a good cause?" he asked himself. But he knew the answer. "They simply can't face it! They can't admit to themselves that the case for miracles is weak or nonexistent." He placed the one-hundred-seventy-three-page report in a binder and glanced at the title page: "Confidential Report on the Evidence for Miracles with Special Reference to the Sixty-Fourth Officially Declared Miracle at Lourdes" by Michael Flanagan, SJ. He put it in his briefcase, picked up his cup of coffee, and gazed out the window.

"Why did I ever accept such a thankless job?" he mused. He remembered as if it were yesterday the cold January morning when Bishop Dwight Thomas, head of what some referred to as "the Catholic Church's Secret Service," summoned Mike to his office. "Mike, I called you in for another special assignment. There is no one in the Church whom I trust as I do you—no one who has your special abilities and expertise." The bishop glanced at the thick dossier on his desk. "Very impressive! Phi Beta Kappa at Yale, Naval intelligence, private investigator. The Church was fortunate indeed when you decided to join the priesthood. And then to top it off, a Harvard Ph.D. with a specialization in Epistemology! I believe that God Himself sent you to us," he said beaming.

Mike thought, "Why is he going through all this again?" He cleared his throat and found himself saying: "I would be willing to help in whatever way I can, of course. But I would like to remind the bishop that I have been working on the Australian exorcism case for several months, and I was hoping that . . ."

"Yes, Mike, I know you expected a vacation," the bishop said, interrupting. "But the superb job you did in Australia convinced me that only you can help us. Exposing Father Collins's 'exorcisms' as fakes is the finest piece of sleuthing I have had the privilege of seeing in almost twenty years in this job. Mind you, many people in the Church hierarchy do not like it. They were hoping that you would find Collins to be legitimate. But your evidence was so convincing that . . . well, never mind that. I have a much more important job for you now, so important I don't think you can refuse."

"You know that I will not refuse," said Mike.

The bishop motioned Mike to have a seat and fixed his eyes on a picture of the Virgin before he started to speak. "As you know, the doctrine that the truth of the Christian religion can be proved on the basis of miracles has been a dogma of the Church since the Third Session of the First Vatican Council in 1870. The Church has maintained that biblical miracles were performed by Moses, the Prophets, Jesus, and others, and even that miracles have occurred in modern times, for example, at Lourdes. The Church has vigorously rejected the view so popular since the nineteenth century that miracles are impossible." The bishop rose from his desk and paced back and forth. "Indeed, St. Pius X in 1910 in the Oath against Modernism maintained that miracles had an enduring apologetic value and said that they were 'eminently suited to the intelligence of all men of every era, including the present.' In fact, the flourishing of the Roman Catholic Church despite hardships and adversities is considered by the Church to be a miracle." He paused and for the first time looked at Mike directly. "However, there are some of our own people who have doubts," he said, his voice growing softer. "They believe that there has been entirely too much emphasis on miracles in the Church's teaching. As people become more educated they find it harder and harder to believe in miracles in the way that the Church expects them to. It may be the case that the doctrine of miracles, far from having a great apologetic value for the Church, may actually contribute to our increasingly bad image. Indeed, some feel that the doctrine of miracles should be de-emphasized and in time perhaps be eliminated altogether. They think that it should not be maintained as a dogma that belief in miracles is rational; thus, perhaps Catholics should believe in some miracles, for example, the Resurrection and the Virgin Birth, but not because these doctrines are rational."

Mike smiled and said, "That sounds like Protestantism to me, Bishop."

"Perhaps, perhaps!" he said, laughing. "I hasten to add," he said, growing serious again, "that this more extreme view is not widely shared and is not likely to be adopted as official Church dogma in our lifetime. Nevertheless, a complete review of the epistemological foundations of belief in miracles is needed. It needs to be done by someone who is Catholic, but who has been trained in some philosophical tradition other than that of St. Thomas Aquinas. The tough appraisal of a Harvard-trained epistemologist is just what is needed. We need especially a critique of the claims of miracles at Lourdes."

"Why Lourdes?" Mike asked.

"Lourdes is unique among Catholic shrines where miracles are supposed to have occurred, since only at Lourdes has there been a definite procedure for investigating and recognizing miracles. If the miracles at Lourdes are found to be suspicious, there will be good reason to be suspicious of other alleged miracles which have not been so rigorously investigated."

"I see," said Mike.

"Of course, I don't mean to anticipate your conclusions. By the way, don't make policy decisions in your report. Just review the epistemological considerations.

"Who will read my report?"

"Well, it will certainly not be made public. I will read it, of course, and so will selected members of my staff. Where it will go from there remains to be seen. For a while it will remain basically confidential, just as your Australian one on exorcism has, although it will have to be much more hush-hush. After that I will have to decide how best to use it strategically and politically. Naturally, you will have the resources of this office at your disposal and a generous expense account for travel and research. I need not remind you that leaks to the press would be intolerable."

"There will be no leaks from this end. But why the rush? I still don't see why I couldn't take a vacation before I . . ."

"I'm sorry, Mike. This is the middle of January. I would like the report on my desk by the first week in June, when there will be a meeting of twelve like-minded members of the Church hierarchy. I am sorry that I cannot tell you more except to say that a critical report on the status of miracles will strengthen the hand of the Twelve. I know that this is not very much time to complete the sort of report I want, so it is important for you to get started at once."

Mike remembered leaving the Bishop's office with mixed feelings. On the one hand, the challenge was exciting. He had always had some reservations about the Church's doctrine of miracles, and this assignment would give him the time and stimulus to test his ideas. On the other hand, knowing the conservative nature of the Church hierarchy, he could not imagine that a report at all critical of the present doctrine would have any effect.

He spent the next two months at libraries reading David Hume's classic critiques of miracles, modern critiques such as that by Antony Flew, and the latest articles on miracles in philosophical and theological journals. With this background, Mike started to investigate the miracles at Lourdes, first by reading some of the classical pro and con literature on the subject and then by investigating the last officially declared miracle at Lourdes—the sixty-fourth officially declared miracle in the history of the shrine. He decided to concentrate on this case because it was the most recent and there would be a greater chance of getting reliable information. This miracle was the alleged cure of Serge Perrin, a French accountant who, while at Lourdes in 1970, experienced a sudden recovery from a long illness. After investigation, the international committee of doctors that investigates the claim of miracles for the Church had said that Perrin was suffering from "a case of recurring organic hemiplegia [paralysis of one side of the body] with ocular lesions, due to cerebral circulatory defects" and that his cure had no medical explanation. By mid-April Mike had read the official dossier on Perrin and the critiques of it, and was ready to begin the less scholarly part of the investigation, the part he liked the best. He traveled to Europe and talked to members of the international committee of doctors who had decided that Perrin's cure was medically inexplicable. He also had Perrin's dossier independently appraised by specialists in the United States. By May he was ready to write.

In mid-May, with the first draft of the report almost done, Mike heard the news. Bishop Thomas had died of a massive heart attack, and with his death his organization had come under close scrutiny. In particular, it was discovered that a confidential report on the miracles was being prepared by Michael Flanagan, SJ, the well known intellectual bloodhound, and the word was out that the powerful men in the Church hierarchy were upset. Toward the end of May, Mike was notified that he should finish his report as quickly as possible and submit it to Monsignor Marcel Pagello, who had taken over Bishop Thomas's responsibilities. He also heard through the grapevine that Pagello was appointed to clean house, and that not much of the old organization in terms either of personnel or ideology would remain when he was finished. Mike could only speculate whether the forthcoming meeting of the mysterious Twelve had been discovered.

When he turned in his report the next morning, Mike was told by the Monsignor's secretary that the Monsignor would spend the day reading it and would see him at 8 A.M. the following day for breakfast. During the day Mike tried to find out all he could about Monsignor Pagello. Few of his contacts knew Pagello very well and the information they had was not helpful. He was described in various ways: "a conservative hard-liner," "brilliant and ruthless," "charming and manipulative." One of Mike's contacts said that in his younger days Pagello was a champion Greco-Roman wrestler, and another spoke of his piercing eyes. Mike decided that he would be completely honest with the Monsignor, tell the truth, stand up for what he believed, and hope for the best.

He knocked on the Monsignor's door promptly at eight and it was immediately opened by a huge bear of a man who said pleasantly, "Father Flanagan, please come in! Can I offer you some coffee and rolls?" while crushing Mike's hand in the most powerful grip he had ever felt. "No thanks, Monsignor. I usually don't eat breakfast."

"Well, please sit down. Let us get right to the point, shall we? I have studied your report on miracles very carefully, and I must say that I am very impressed by the scholarship and thought that have gone into it. However, the position that you take in the report is quite unacceptable to the Church because it conflicts with our doctrines. It would be unfortunate if it ever became known that the Church had actually sponsored this report. So I must ask you to refrain from ever revealing—and I underline the word 'ever'—that it was sponsored by this office or by any office of the Church."

"Yes, Monsignor, I will agree to that."

"Good, good! I deem it regrettable that Bishop Thomas and others saw fit to use the resources of this office to instigate heretical and unorthodox ideas. Although Bishop Thomas's death was a tragic loss to the Church, he had recently taken a course of action that could only have led to unfortunate consequences. Had he not died he would have had to be replaced. We had been watching him for some time and . . ."

"But what about the merits of my argument?" Mike asked, interrupting. "I believe that what I said was true."

"Yes, I am sure you do. What in particular do you think is true in your report?"

"First of all, if you recall, I argue that even if miracles have occurred, when 'miracle' is defined as an event caused by some noncorporeal creature, their existence gives no support to belief in God. A noncorporeal creature need not be God. There are rival supernatural hypotheses that account for miracles as well as the God hypothesis."

"Yes, I noted with interest that you adopted the concept of miracles used by Pope Benedict XIV in his classic treatise *De servorum Dei beatificatione et beatorum cononizatione,* in which a miracle need only be beyond the powers of corporeal creatures. However, just because miracles can be caused by created spirits who are not God, for example, angels, they would still be produced by God in the sense that the created spirit acted as God's agent."

"I am afraid, Monsignor, that you do not understand the radical nature of my thesis. My point is not that angels could be the direct cause of miracles. Miracles could be caused by noncorporeal beings that are not God's agents. God and angels might not exist although other supernatural beings might. For example, polytheism might be true and, if so, it, as well as theism, would account for miracles. I am not suggesting that polytheism is true, of course, only that the existence of miracles even as defined by Pope Benedict XIV is compatible with it."

"I see," the Monsignor said quietly. Mike was not sure that he did see, or that if he did, he wanted to.

"However, my main argument is that in order to claim that a miracle has occurred, rival hypotheses must be shown to be less probable than the miracle hypothesis. For example, the miracle-hypothesis explanation of some event must be shown to be more probable than the hypothesis that the event will be explained by future science utilizing as yet undiscovered laws that govern nature. Given the scientific progress of the last two centuries, such a prediction seems rash and unjustified. In medicine, for example, diseases that were considered mysterious are now understood without appeal to supernatural powers. Further progress seems extremely likely; indeed, it seems plausible to suppose that many so-called miracle cures of the past will one day be understood, as some have already been, in terms of psychosomatic medicine."

"Would you make that same claim about the Resurrection? Will your science some day explain how our Lord rose from the dead?" the monsignor said, his voice dripping with sarcasm.

"I don't think one can rule that out," Mike replied, getting up from his chair. "However, there are other hypotheses that must be eliminated that are perhaps more relevant in the case of the Resurrection and some other biblical miracles. The difficulties of ruling out hoax, fraud, or deception are legend. We have excellent reason today to believe that some contemporary faith healers use fraud and deceit to make it seem that they have paranormal powers and are getting miracle cures and even resurrecting people from the dead. These men have little trouble in duping a public that is surely no less sophisticated than that of biblical times. Did Jesus really walk on the water or only appear to because he was walking on rocks below the surface? Did Jesus turn the water into wine or did he only appear to because he substituted wine for water by some clever trick? Did Jesus arise from the dead or did his disciples make it seem as if he did? The hypothesis that Jesus was a magician has been seriously considered by some biblical scholars. The success of some contemporary 'faith healers' and 'psychic wonders' in convincing the public of 'miracle cures' by the use of deception and fraud indicates that it was possible for Jesus, if he was a magician, to do the same."

"How can you believe in God and say these things, Father!" exclaimed the monsignor, with a touch of anguish in his voice.

"Again I think you misunderstand me. I am not doubting the divinity of Jesus, but only that this can be demonstrated by miracles," Mike said, taking his seat again. "There is still another hypothesis that is a rival to the miracle hypothesis. Alleged miracles may not be due to some trick or fraud, but to misperceptions based on religious bias. A person full of religious zeal may see what he or she wants to see, not what is really there. We know from empirical studies that people's beliefs and prejudices influence what they see and report. It would not be surprising that religious people who report that they have seen miraculous events have projected their biases onto the actual event. Did Jesus still the storm as it is claimed in the Gospel according to Matthew, or did the storm by coincidence happen to stop when 'He rose and rebuked the wind and the sea' and witnesses in their religious zeal 'saw' Him stilling the storm?"

"No doubt this sometimes happens. But to suppose that religious believers are not able to separate true from false miracles seems implausible," the monsignor said.

"But why? Religious attitudes often foster uncritical belief and acceptance. Indeed, in a religious context, uncritical belief is often thought to be a virtue, with doubt and skepticism a vice. Thus, a belief arising in a religious context and held with only modest conviction may tend to reinforce itself and develop into an unshakable conviction. It would hardly be surprising if, in this context, some ordinary natural event were seen as a miracle."

The monsignor did not reply. With a grim expression on his face he rose from his chair and began leafing through the report.

"I also believe that my analysis of the Perrin case

at Lourdes is correct," Mike said. "Here one question was whether the international committee which determined that the cure was medically inexplicable was competent to decide such issues. At best, this committee had only the competence to decide that the cure was scientifically inexplicable in terms of current knowledge of nature. This committee did not know what the future development of medical science would be; thus any judgment that the committee made about the absolute inexplicability of a cure in terms of nature can and should have no particular authority."

The monsignor looked at Mike with eyes that seemed to penetrate to his soul. "I need not remind you, Father Flanagan, that the final authority for the judgment that a cure at Lourdes is a miracle is made by the Church. If the majority of the committee decides that the cure is inexplicable, the patient's dossier is given to the canonical commission headed by the bishop of the diocese in which the allegedly cured person lives. Only the Church can make the final decision as to whether the event is a miracle; that is, whether God has intervened in the natural course of events."

"Yes, I am quite aware of that and, in fact, I consider that in my report—I think around page 150. My point is that even if it was caused by some supernatural force or forces, this need not be caused by the Christian God. Church officials who make the final decision about whether a cure is a miracle and if so, whether it is caused by God, apparently ignore these other alternatives. As a result, the final decision that the cure is explained by God's intervention is more like a leap of faith than a rational decision. Further, the decisions of the Church are contingent on the competence of the international committee of doctors. But, as I have already argued, this committee's judgment exceeded its competence."

"I gather you have reservations about the committee's actual application of present-day medical knowledge," said the monsignor, again glancing through the report.

"Yes, my investigation indicated that the committee should not have concluded what it did. A small sample of specialists in the United States who independently examined the document produced by the international committee of doctors found the cure of Perrin very suspicious, the data in the document highly problematic, and the document obscure and filled with technical verbiage. For example, although crucial laboratory tests such as a spinal tap and radiation brain scan were standard in most hospitals for diagnosing the illness Perrin was said to have, they were never performed. The reviewers also considered the diagnosis of hemiplegia very implausible since, because he had right leg weakness and left visual and motor symptoms, more than one side of Perrin's brain had to be involved. In addition, symptoms of generalized constriction of his visual field and various sensory motor disturbances suggested hysteria rather than an organic illness. Moreover, the American specialists who reviewed the document maintained that if there was an organic illness at all, multiple sclerosis was the most likely explanation of Perrin's symptoms. However, it is well known that multiple sclerosis has fleeting symptoms with periodic severe flare-ups followed by remissions that are sometimes complete."

The monsignor looked up as if he expected Mike to say more. Mike continued: "As I also point out, there were serious problems not only with the investigation of the Perrin case, but with the sixty-third officially declared miracle as well. The problems with both cases suggest that there is something badly amiss in the application of the procedures used by the Catholic Church for declaring something a miracle cure at Lourdes. An apparently questionable diagnosis of Perrin and an unsubstantiated judgment about the cure involved in the sixty-third official miracle were accepted by the Lourdes medical bureau and the international committee."

The monsignor glanced at his watch. "Well, this has been most edifying, Father Flanagan! But I am afraid that another matter forces me to bring our pleasant chat to an end. Is there any final statement that you would like to make?"

"Only this. Although I believe that I show in the report that belief in miracles is not rationally justifiable, I don't mean to suggest that the Church should give up maintaining that miracles have occurred. I believe the uneducated members of our Church need to believe in miracles and that we should, for their sake, keep up the pretense that the miracles are rationally justified. But we who are educated and enlightened should not maintain this view. Indeed, we should believe in miracles on faith and faith alone. I further . . ."

"Thank you, Father," the monsignor interrupted. "Your ideas are interesting and will be taken into account when I make my decision about what to do with your report," he said, rising from his chair, smiling.

"What are the possible dispositions of my report?" Mike asked.

"The most likely disposition will be for it to be put in the archives in one of our libraries for scholarly use. Of course, it will have few readers. But we shall see! Thank you again, Father Flanagan," he said as he showed Mike to the door.

That night in his room Mike prayed as he never had before. God seemed close and intimate, like a brother or loved one. Mike still believed in miracles despite his report. He passionately believed in the Resurrection, the Virgin Birth, the feeding of the five hundred, and the rest. Indeed, he believed more firmly than before he had written the report. But how could he? The evidence was against them! They were improbable in the light of the facts. How could he, who was trained in logic and reason, who argued the importance of epistemic responsibility, believe in them? He thanked God for his belief despite the evidence and despite his training and commitment to reason. His belief was itself a miracle of sorts. He wept for joy and was reminded of a well-known passage from Hume's *Essay Concerning Human Understanding*:

> [The] Christian religion not only was at first attended with miracles, but even to this day cannot be believed by any reasonable person without them. Mere reason is not sufficient to convince us of its veracity; and whoever is moved by faith to assent to it is conscious of a continued miracle in his own person, which subverts all the principles of his understanding, and gives him a determination to believe what is most contrary to custom and experience.

A week after his meeting with the Monsignor, Father Michael Flanagan received notification of his next assignment. For an indefinite time he was to teach English in a small Catholic college in Iowa. He learned some time later that the "Confidential Report on the Evidence for Miracles with Special Reference to the Sixty-Fourth Officially Declared Miracle at Lourdes," by Michael Flanagan, SJ, had been placed in the archives of Catholic University of America, where it was read by two graduate students.

Frenchy's Con

Subway Slim and Fast Eddie were trying to work the old horse race scam outta 'Frisco back in '46 when they first met him. Things weren't going good. The suckers weren't biting and Slim was getting mighty discouraged.

"Gee, Eddie, with the way things are goin' we might hafta turn legit for a while to make a livin'," Slim said one day.

"Slim, I don't wanna ever hear ya talk that way 'gain," said Eddie. "A good con man can always make a livin'. Turnin' legit just ain't in the cards for the likes of us. We just gotta find a new con."

"Eddie, I been in this racket for near twenty years an' I ain't seen a new con yet. They're all variations on oldies."

Slim was wrong. That very night they met Frenchy. That's not his real name, of course, but that's what they called him and he didn't seem to mind. It happened this way. Slim and Eddie were in a bar in 'Frisco looking for some likely suckers when they met him. He was dressed fit to kill in a fancy suit and long hair like he was going to some costume party or something.

"Monsieurs," he said as he bowed low, "mey I bay yoo a dreenk?"

You could tell right away he was from foreign parts 'cause he talked sort of funny and acted like he was on the stage or something. Slim and Eddie looked at each other hoping that maybe they had found their sucker. But before they knew what had happened, Frenchy was talking to them about God and such stuff. He said that you couldn't prove that God existed. Slim and Eddie sure believed that since they didn't believe in God at all. Slim claimed that he never had and Eddie gave up believing when his Uncle Ben—better known as Beneficent Ben—was killed by cancer. "Best damn con man I ever knew," he would say. But then Frenchy said something that caught Eddie's notice, although he wasn't sure Slim picked up on it right away. Frenchy said that belief in God was still the best bet and said that for five bucks he would tell them why they should believe. Without blinking an eye, Slim gave him a five spot. Frenchy used a lot of fancy words to explain it but what it came down to was this: If you believe God exists and He does, then you go to Heaven. In other words, you get what Beneficent Ben used to call the Pie in the Sky. If you believe God exists and God doesn't, then so what? You lose some small change and that's all. However, if you don't believe in God, and He does exist, you go to Hell, which is pretty damn scary. But if He doesn't exist and you don't believe in Him, you get chicken feed. Only a sucker wouldn't believe in God and who wants to be a sucker?

Slim acted really impressed with what Frenchy said. But he said that he didn't see how he could start believing in God after all these years. "Frenchy, there's an expression we have in English: Ya can't teach an ol' dog new tricks," Slim said.

Frenchy let it be known that there was such a similar expression in his language too, but he had a way around it: "une methode" he called it. He said for another fiver he would tell all. Slim again came through. Frenchy said that belief in God could be developed by acting in pious ways, for example, by attending mass, taking the sacraments and other such things that churchgoers do. Slim said right off that he was going to start going to mass tomorrow and thanked old Frenchy for his help. Frenchy looked pleased.

When Slim and Eddie were alone they looked at each other and laughed! "What a great con, Eddie," said Slim, lowering his voice. "It's worth ten bucks."

"Yeah, it's so simple and so persuasive," Eddie said.

"If ya bet on the Big Guy in the Sky an' win, ya win everythin', an' if ya lose, ya ain't out much!" Slim said.

"But if ya bet agin' the Big Guy an' ya lose, ya lose everythin' an' if ya bet on the Big Guy an' lose, ya lose peanuts!" Eddie added.

"This is gotta be the greatest con of all time," said Slim.

"There's more holes in the argument than a piece of Swiss cheese! What about if the Big Guy hated jerks tryin' to get to Heaven in that way an' reserved a place in Hell for 'em?" Eddie whooped.

"What about if there's a Big Gal instead of a Big Guy in the Sky who sent any stupe t'Hell who believed in the Big Guy?" Slim said gleefully.

Not to be outdone, Eddie said: "What about if the Big Guy in the Sky was not God but some Bastard who sent anyone t'Hell who believed in any god at'll!"

They spent the next fifteen minutes giving funnier and funnier examples until their sides ached from laughing. Finally Slim said, "But, Eddie, if we can see all of these problems with what Frenchy said, maybe the suckers will too."

"Sure, some of them will. But that's true of all good cons. The question is whether some will bite an' my guess is that for sure a lot will. Uncle Ben always taught me that a good con 'peals to a sucker's selfishness an' it must 'pear to be safe. Frenchy's con fits the bill! Unless ya look close it seems safe as Hell and it sure 'peals to human selfishness: Get the Pie in the Sky for Number One!" said Eddie.

"Sure it's a great con, Eddie, but can we use it? Is there any way we can adopt it to our operation?"

Eddie thought a long time on this one. "Slim, I wish like blazes that we could. I thought me an' you might get ourselves hired out by some church. We could use the con t'get members for the church an' the church would pay us by the head. But with our record I kind of doubt that a 'spectable church would hire us. Besides preachers and such types might have been using this con already. 'Though it is new to the likes of us it might have been 'round for a long time."

"What about startin' our own church?" Slim suggested.

"Think of the members we could get usin' Frenchy's con! Even jerks who had strayed from the fold an' who no longer believed could be brung back for the salvation of Number One! I bet 'though Frenchy's con has been used before it has never been the main drawing card. In our church it would be. We could get phony divinity degrees, develop a new spiel . . ."

And so, Subway Slim and Fast Eddie talked on into the night. When Eddie thought back, he wasn't sure why Slim and he never followed through: Fear of starting a brand new con was probably the biggest thing. Ten years later Subway Slim's pumper gave out and after that Fast Eddie worked solo until he retired. But whenever he saw those phony preachers on the boob tube and read about the moola that they made it sort of made him wonder. "Could Subway Slim and me have made it big as TV preachers using Frenchy's con?" he often wondered. Eddie never saw Frenchy again. However, Eddie did often think: "I do believe that if the con was his idea, the guy was a real genius. Why, he may have been an even better con man than my Uncle Ben!"

Dear Mom

Dunster House
Harvard University
Oct. 1

Dear Mom:

Sorry about not writing. I moved into Dunster House last week and I like it a lot. What a change from the freshman dorms! I have some interesting roommates. Joe is a musician from Canada who plays the violin and is majoring in philosophy, Carl is a history major from Cleveland who always seems to have his nose in a book. Then there is Paul. Paul is a very strange guy, but I like him a lot. He prays a lot and wants me to read the Bible with him. So far I haven't had time. But he is very persistent. It is too early to tell about my classes, but the Soc. Sci. prof is very funny. I will probably go out for wrestling and I am starting to get in shape. I will write soon. Love to Susan.

Love,
Bobby

P.S.: How is your writing going? I have not told any of my roommates yet that my mother is the famous writer, Ann Larson. I don't know how much longer I should wait!

* * *

New York City
Oct. 4

Dear Bobby:

It was wonderful to hear from you, Darling! But your letter was so brief! This mother and famous writer would appreciate longer epistles from her only son. I would love to learn more about your roommates, especially Paul. I would be very interested to hear about what you think of his religious pitch. Your father insisted on not giving you or Susie any religious instruction and in a way I believe he was correct. However, it does create a vacuum that can become too easily filled. Take care that your Paul does not become "St. Paul!"

Your wrestling plans sound very good. Yes, you must keep in shape! Let it be known that your old mom is taking judo lessons at the health club and in a few months may be ready to take on her muscular son! Why judo? Well, since your father's death I have felt a wee bit unprotected. Would it be an embarrassment to you if your mom earned a black belt? Then you really would have something to keep secret!

Susie and I are terribly proud of you. I know your father would be too. Write soon.

Love,
Mom

* * *

Dunster House
Harvard University
Oct. 20

Dear Mom:

Well, I hope this will not be a shock, but I have started to read the New Testament with Paul and I am also praying with him. Yes, perhaps you are right about there being a vacuum in my religious education. I feel good about it and Paul says that I must commit myself to Christ passionately and without reservation. Paul says we are not really alive until we accept Christ. I have been trying to keep up with my classwork but my religious education takes a lot of my time. I decided that I may not go out for wrestling after all. Your judo lessons sound good. I hope you don't get hurt getting tossed all over the place. If you feel unprotected, perhaps you need Christ too. Paul says that Jesus is the best protection anyone can get. Think about it! Love to Susan.

Love,
Bobby

* * *

New York City
Oct. 21

Dear Bobby:

Well, your last epistle was no longer than the first, but it packed much more of a punch! Its effect on me was something like being slammed to the mat by Professor Konyono (my judo teacher). I can see that Paul has indeed become St. Paul despite my warning! By all means commit yourself passionately to Christ, Darling, but please find out what you are getting into before you do. For example, have you checked to see whether Christianity is true? Or would its falsehood not stand in the way of your being passionately committed? As you must know, Christianity is based on certain historical claims: that Jesus was a historical figure, that he arose from the dead, that he was born of a virgin, and so on. Is there good evidence for these claims? Perhaps your other roommate, Carl, the one who is the history major, could be prevailed upon to get his nose out of a book long enough to suggest something for you to read concerning the historical veracity of what you are about to be committed to. Susie read your last letter and told me to tell you that she will still love you if you become a "Jesus freak" but she would never speak to you again. On the other hand, your old mom will continue to speak to you and love you but will be sorely disappointed if you don't keep up with your schoolwork. Please, Darling, don't waste your time at Harvard.

While my dear son slacks off in his wrestling training, his old mom has just earned her yellow belt. Professor Konyono says that I have talent and he will enter me in the novice competition in a few weeks. I have developed a devastating *osoto gari*—a leaping throw—in which I dispatch even the biggest men in class. I'm sure your father would think this very amusing. However, he always tried to encourage me to take up a sport. Write soon!

Love,
Mom

P.S.: I am afraid that I must decline the offer to make Christ my protector. He seemed even unable to protect himself from his enemies in his last days. In a dark alley with potential assailants closing in I would prefer to have Professor Konyono at my side.

* * *

Dunster House
Harvard University
Nov. 10

Dear Mom:

I talked to Carl and he did recommend some books. It turns out that he knows a lot about biblical scholarship himself. He says it is one of his hobbies. My conversation with Carl and the little reading I have done have convinced me that the historical basis of Christianity is pretty flimsy. The major source of evidence for the main doctrines is from the New Testament, and Carl and the books I have read point out that these doctrines have not been independently verified (Carl's term!) by pagan and Jewish sources. In fact, there are some scholars who think that Jesus is a myth. Carl also pointed out to me last night that the evidence to support many of the claims of Christianity needs to be especially strong since the claims are of miraculous events that are initially incredible. (Carl's term again!) But far from being strong, the evidence is weak. For example, Carl showed me the various inconsistencies in the New Testament resurrection story. Unfortunately, I have had to read these books and talk to Carl when Paul is not around. Paul says all of this historical evidence is irrelevant to Christianity and he gets mad when you bring it up. He says that tomorrow night he will have a long talk with me and explain why.

Yes, I agree that Dad would have liked the idea of your taking judo. He always said that you were the most athletic member of the family, not to mention the smartest! Tell Susan I will still love her even if she will not speak to me.

Love,
Bobby

* * *

New York City
Nov. 12

Dear Bobby:

Your last epistle gladdened your old mom's heart! You sound like you are thinking again. Carl sounds like a gem. I didn't tell you, but I have been boning up on biblical scholarship just in case Carl didn't come through. What he says sounds exactly right! Keep me posted, Darling!

I am a little stuck in my writing. My editor is very encouraging, of course, but sometimes the creative juices simply do not flow. What should I do? Does my favorite son have any advice to offer his old mom to get them flowing again? Have an affair? Remarry? Practice transcendental meditation? Climb mountains?

By the way, Susie is a great comfort. Such a sensible and loving sister you have, Bobby! You must know that she admires her big brother enormously, but she does worry about you. I hope she has no need to. Susie and I talk of you often and miss you.

Love,
Mom

* * *

New York City
Nov. 30

Dear Bobby:

Darling, is everything all right? It has been some time since I have heard from you. I am beginning to worry. Please let me know what is happening.

I won my first judo match! It was a tremendous thrill. I was matched against a young woman from the rival *dojo*—school of judo—and I threw her with my dreaded *de ashi barai*—a foot sweep. Professor Konyono was very kind and said that my foot sweep was "perfect." He said I must do more *randori*—the equivalent of sparring in boxing—to sharpen my skill.

The other piece of good news is that my writing is starting to flow again. I don't know why. Perhaps you sent me good vibes from Cambridge. As always, Susie sends her love.

Love,
Mom

* * *

Dunster House
Harvard University
Dec. 1

Dear Mom:

I have been a little afraid to write you since I know you will disapprove of what I have done. I have accepted Jesus as my Savior. I understand all of the historical problems, but Paul has convinced me that this does not matter. Paul says that one must make a leap of faith and believe despite the evidence. You must completely disregard any doubts that you might have. Paul says that a person with faith is not unaware of the possibility of error in such a commitment, but is not anxious because of this. Mom, Paul calls the kind of reasoning that you and Carl use objective reasoning. A person with faith knows that according to objective reasoning, belief in God is not justified. Nevertheless, it is just because it is not based on objective reasoning that faith is the highest virtue. Paul says that with objective certainty comes lack of personal growth and spiritual stagnation. But with faith there is risk, danger, and adventure—all essential for spiritual growth and transcendence. Paul argues that total and passionate commitment to God, even when it seems absurd, is necessary for human salvation and ultimately for human happiness. So, Mom, Paul has convinced me to reject your appeal to historical evidence to substantiate the claims of Christianity. That is really beside the point.

I'm sorry, Mom. Have I disappointed you? I guess I have become a "Jesus freak" after all. I feel good—almost as if I am on a high. I hope Susan will still speak to me. Paul and I are thinking of dropping out of Harvard and devoting ourself to spreading the Good News.

Yours in Christ,
Bobby

* * *

New York City
Dec. 2

Dear Bobby:

No, Darling, I am not disappointed. But I am concerned. I so want the best for you. I wonder if you have thought through the implications of Paul's counsel. Paul's advice seems personally and socially dangerous. Consider the personal implications. Should one cancel all of one's insurance policies if one has faith that one will live forever, despite the evidence to the contrary? Applying Paul's advice to me, perhaps I should sell all of the stocks and bonds that your father left us and give the money to Uncle Harry to invest for me—you know Harry, the one whose investments always go sour—since I have faith, despite the historical record, that Harry will come through. Or perhaps I should become a member of a local satanic cult. Why? Because I have faith, despite the absurdity of the views of the cult, that they are true. Surely you can see that just because I believe passionately and completely that I will live forever, that Harry's investments will turn out well, and that Satan is our Savior, that this is irrelevant to what I should do.

Paul's advice is also socially dangerous, since it can lead to fanaticism. If I can believe in satanic cult absurdities, Nazis can believe in their absurdities. The historical record indicates that fanaticism is one of the greatest scourges of humankind and has had horrible consequences. Of course, all of my arguments rely on the historical evidence which Paul seems to reject. Are you really prepared to reject this evidence too, Bobby? Darling, thanks again for your letter. Please reconsider what you are doing. Susie sends her love.

Love,
Mom

* * *

Dunster House
Harvard University
Dec. 5

Dear Mom:

I'm sorry you are taking my religious commitment so hard. Your letter was very painful for me to read. I showed it to Paul and he said there was a big difference between faith in Christ and faith in the other things that you brought up and that you were being unfair. I feel torn between what you were getting at in your letter—the complete irrationality of it all—and the sort of feeling I get from talking to Paul and reading Scripture. I guess I am confused. I am going away for the holidays with Joe, who lives in Canada, to try to sort things out. My love to Susan. How is your judo coming along?

Love,
Bobby

* * *

New York City
Dec. 8

Dear Bobby:

Darling, thanks your latest letter. What you say suggests that my arguments might have had some effect. Please think about what Paul said in response to them. Paul says that "there was a big difference between faith in Christ and faith in the other things that you brought up," does he? Darling, my point is that there is no difference. I notice that you don't say that Paul has told you what it is. Did you ask him?

I have never told you this before, Bobby, but when I was a young woman I too had a deep religious commitment. It lasted for several years. I sought solitude in the woods and tried to communicate with God. I found only silence. It cured me of religion forever. You too must make up your own mind. I just want to be sure you know what your own mind is and are thinking clearly.

Susie and I are disappointed without measure that you will not be coming home for the holidays. Susie got teary when she heard the news. I have not heard much about Joe except that he is a musician. What will you do? Where will you go in Canada?

Your old mom continues to excel in judo. I have now perfected my *uchi mata*—an inside thigh sweep. Professor Konyono says that I should get a brown belt very soon. Susie and I both miss you terribly.

Love,
Mom

* * *

Dunster House
Harvard University
Jan. 8

Dear Mom:

Well, Joe and I are back from Canada. Joe lives in Calgary and we did lots of cross-country skiing and snowshoeing in the Canadian Rockies. It was great fun and I had a lot of time to think about religion and commitment. I got to know Joe very well, too. I like him a lot, perhaps more than any of my other roommates. He is a sensible and low-key guy who never gets excited. Naturally, I told him about my religious concerns. He did not tell me what he believes, and after listening patiently to my problems, he said that I would have to make up my own mind. He sounds like you! Since Joe is a philosophy major, he put it in terms of what he called epistemic responsibility. He said that I had to decide whether I was going to believe on the basis of the evidence and be epistemically responsible or whether I was not going to be. I guess I have decided on epistemic responsibility.

I was prepared to confront Paul and have it out when I returned. I wasn't sure whether he and I could be friends after this. But I did not have to worry. Paul has left school. When Joe and I returned, his books and belongings were gone from the room. There was no note or anything. Carl said that Paul was failing his classes, so that may have had something to do with it. Anyway, he is gone and, although I will miss him, I am relieved.

I am afraid my grades for the first semester may not be very good. I am very much behind, although I am making a serious effort to make up for lost time. I have started wrestling again and am I out of shape! The coach said that I will have to work hard to catch up.

Oh, I forgot to tell you the big news about Joe. He knows judo. Yes, he has a black belt! Was he ever impressed and surprised to find out about you! He said that he wished his mom knew judo. Tell Susan I will be home between semesters and that I miss her.

Love,
Bobby

* * *

New York City
Jan. 15

Dear Bobby:

My son, my son, how you never fail to surprise me! Epistemic responsibility no less! I am sorry to hear about Paul, although Harvard may not have been the right place for him. What do you think? About your grades: Grades are not everything and I have a hunch that you learned a thing or two this semester that is more important than an entire Harvard education.

Wrestle hard, Darling! I am delighted to see you are back. The news about Joe is astounding. He sounds wonderful! Please bring him home over the semester break. Susie and I would love to meet him. With Susie on the cello and Joe on the violin and your old mom on the piano we would have a world-class trio! I promise I will not embarrass you by asking Joe to *randori* with me at the *dojo*.

I have completed the first draft of my MS and I am

starting on revisions. Susie and I are delighted and thrilled that we will see you soon.

Love,
Mom

P.S.: You cannot imagine who stopped by on his way to "a new assignment." Remember your cousin Michael Flanagan? The brilliant one? He received Phi Beta Kappa from Yale, went into Naval intelligence, and then became a private investigator. He shocked everyone in the family by converting to Catholicism and then going into the priesthood. He went on to get a Ph.D. in Philosophy from Harvard. He is very close-mouthed about what he does. However, I gather from Aunt Beth that he does sleuthing for the Church. I surmise from my brief visit with him that unlike most Catholics, he rejects the traditional arguments for God and bases his belief on faith. I am sure Paul and he would get along famously!

* * *

New York City
Feb. 3

Dear Bobby:

What a wonderful visit! It was absolutely delightful to have Joe here. He is such a fine young person. I must report that your sister Susie was completely captivated and now says that she is applying to Radcliffe. This, despite her saying for years that she would rather die than go to her old mom's alma mater. Being near Joe aside, I think Radcliffe would be just right for her. She is so intellectual and I think she would like Cambridge. Please write to her, Bobby. She has great confidence in your judgment.

Joe mentioned in passing that you and he might be taking a philosophy course together next semester. Is this because of your encounter with Paul? To guard against new St. Pauls that you might encounter? In any case, it is a fine idea and I approve whole-heartedly. Susie says she will major in philosophy if she goes to Radcliffe. I can't imagine why!

I thought I should tell you and not keep it a secret any longer that your old mom is starting to date (do they use that term anymore?) a very nice man I met in judo class. After I threw him with a splendid *uchi mata* it was almost love at first sight. His name is Fred Beneke. He is a doctor, a widower, and unlike so many doctors, is very intellectual. Would you believe he actually read my work! He goes to Boston often to visit his daughter and perhaps I will go with him the next time. Is the news too much of a shock for you? Susie seemed very pleased and only said: "Well, Mom, it's about time!"

Love,
Mom

Part IV

God-Rejection

The Sermon by the Sea

With his back toward the tranquil sea, the Preacher with No Name addressed the crowd. The five theologians stood imposingly in their black academic gowns on the fringes of the group. They were silent as the preacher spoke passionately about God-Fall; they fidgeted nervously as he vigorously advocated God-Rejection; they frowned and whispered among themselves as he loudly proclaimed the goal of God-Free. If the preacher was aware of their presence, he did not show it.

Finally, the oldest and largest of the theologians stepped forward and said loudly, "The Preacher with No Name says that one should reject God. But he gives no reasons for this remarkable doctrine. Perhaps he would tell us why." Then, the smallest and youngest of the theologians spoke: "Yes, the Preacher with No Name proclaims the goal of freedom from

God that goes against the traditions of our religion, and yet provides no reasons for his views! Why should anyone believe him?"

There was a loud murmur in the crowd. The preacher heard it and answered: "I am pleased that my distinguished listeners from the university ask questions. However, if they had been at the Commons yesterday and heard me speak, they would not have needed to ask these questions."

"Answer again!" several members of the crowd shouted.

"Very well," the preacher said. "The five gentlemen from the university say that I do not give reasons for my views of God-Rejection and for the goal of God-Free. But the shoe should be on the other foot. The burden of proof is surely on them to tell us why we should accept God and live a life committed to God. As we all know, the arguments for the existence of God are either weak or invalid. Indeed, some of the distinguished gentlemen from the university have written learned papers that show the fallacies involved in these arguments. Why should anyone believe in God given this situation? They do not tell us except to say that acceptance of God is part of your religious tradition. But so what? The tradition might be wrong. My friends, why should we believe the distinguished gentlemen from the university who say that God exists?"

A dark-skinned theologian stepped forward, carrying several bound volumes under his arm, and spoke in a quiet manner. "The Preacher with No Name makes a valid point. But he should be reminded that he advocates not only that people should not believe in God, but that they should disbelieve in God. For this latter claim he must show more than that the burden of proof is on us. He must give positive reasons for not believing. We await his arguments."

The Preacher smiled at this response and said: "I will be happy to provide reasons for disbelief, but some of these are of such a nature that only the gentlemen from the university will understand them. Will my friends indulge me and allow me to speak to them in their own terms?"

"Yes, yes!" came the reply from the crowd.

After a brief pause he asked, "What do the gentlemen from the university mean by 'God'?"

A theologian with a red face and bright yellow hair stepped forward and said: "I think that we all agree that God is a disembodied being who is all-knowing, all-powerful, morally perfect, and completely free."

"Will the gentlemen from the university agree that such a being cannot exist if the idea of a disembodied being who is all-knowing, all-powerful, morally perfect, and completely free is contradictory?" the preacher asked.

The theologians nodded their heads.

"Good! Let us consider the claim that God is all-knowing. This implies that He has all of the knowledge that there is. But what would this mean? There are at least three different kinds of knowledge. First, there is factual knowledge. This is knowledge that something is the case and is usually understood as true belief of a certain kind. Next, there is knowledge how. This is a type of skill and is not reducible to factual knowledge. In particular, knowledge how is not simply factual knowledge of how things work or how to do things. One might have factual knowledge of how to swim, and yet lack the physical skill to do so. Knowledge how as I use it refers to possession of the skill. Finally, there is knowledge by acquaintance. This is direct acquaintance with some object, person, or phenomenon. So if God is all-knowing, He not only knows every fact but he has every type of knowledge how, and for every aspect of every entity in the universe, He has direct acquaintance of it."

The five theologians listened carefully to the preacher's words.

"But the property of being all-knowing in this sense is incompatible with God's disembodiedness and with his moral perfection." The preacher paused and continued. "For example, God's disembodiedness is incompatible with his knowing how to swim and other physical skills. In order to swim one must have a body, but God by definition does not."

The youngest and smallest of the theologians spoke, his voice shaking. "The Preacher with No Name's definition of all-knowing is unacceptable! God can only have knowledge that it is logically possible for Him to have. Of course, God cannot know how to swim since it is logically impossible for Him to do so. Do not ask God to do the impossible!"

The preacher answered him thus: "I wonder if the gentleman from the university has thought this reply through, since it has strange and paradoxical implications. One normally supposes that if a person is all-knowing, then this person has knowledge that any being has who is not all-knowing. Furthermore, one normally supposes that if God exists, God has all knowledge that humans have. But both these suppositions are false on the gentleman's account. Human beings can know how to swim and human beings are not all-knowing. Yet God cannot have this knowledge!"

The five theologians whispered among themselves.

Finally, the only one who had not spoken so far stepped forward. He was tall and ungainly and spoke in a breathless and nervous manner. "The Preacher with No Name has no doubt forgotten that it is our belief that Our Lord became incarnated in Jesus, a human being. In this form God could have had the 'knowledge how' of which you make so much." So saying he stepped back and cast his eyes downward.

"No, I have not forgotten about the story of Jesus, the Man-God. But this hardly solves the problem. Before Jesus' incarnation, God was still considered to be all-knowing. God not did become all-knowing after God became flesh, did He?" Before any of the theologians could come forward again, the preacher continued, "But this is not the only inconsistency. There are many others. If God is all-knowing, He has knowledge by acquaintance of all aspects of lust and envy. But one aspect of lust and envy is feeling lust and envy. However, part of the idea of God is that He is morally perfect, and being morally perfect excludes these feelings. Consequently, there is another contradiction in the idea of God. God, because He is all-knowing, must experience the feelings of lust and envy. But God, because He is morally perfect, is excluded from doing so."

The oldest and largest theologian spoke angrily. "Preacher with No Name, let it be known that God's moral goodness does not concern His feelings but rather His actions and the principles on which they rest, and so the fact that He knows lust and envy does not affect the moral ideal."

"I think not," said the preacher calmly. "We would not consider a person morally perfect, despite a life of good actions, if there were envy and lust in his or her heart. Freedom from such feelings is precisely what religious believers expect of a saint, and it is inconceivable that God would be less morally perfect than a saint. Surely the gentlemen from the university would agree!"

As the five theologians spoke softly among themselves, the preacher continued: "Perhaps my learned listeners would like to consider another contradiction. Since God is all-powerful, He cannot experience fear, frustration, and despair. For in order to have these experiences one must believe that one is limited in power. But since God is all-knowing and all-powerful, He knows that He is not limited in power. Consequently, He cannot have complete knowledge by acquaintance of all aspects of fear, frustration, and despair. But since He is all-knowing, He must have this knowledge by acquaintance."

The tall ungainly theologian spoke: "The Preacher with No Name is mistaken to believe that although God is all-powerful, He cannot experience fear and frustration. After all, even humans sometimes experience fear when they know that they have nothing to fear. If, given their limitations, humans can do this, surely God without these limitations can do so as well. He can experience fear although He knows He has absolutely nothing to fear."

The preacher smiled and said: "In ordinary life, although we are afraid when we know we have nothing to fear, we also have a belief, perhaps an unconscious one, that there is something to fear. Indeed, if we did not have such a belief, it would be strange to speak of our state as one of fear. Even God must believe He has something to fear if He experiences fear. But He cannot believe He has something to fear if He is all-knowing. However, let us suppose that it is possible that someone can experience fear knowing that they have nothing to fear. Surely in this case we can say that this person's fear is irrational. By definition God cannot be irrational."

"My colleagues want to confer with one another," said the dark theologian who carried the bound volumes under his arms.

"Very well. The gentlemen from the university can confer as long as they wish!" replied the preacher. In a few moments the largest and oldest theologian came forward and said, "At the present time we cannot find anything wrong with the Preacher with No Name's arguments given the definition of 'all-knowing' proposed and thus find it necessary to reject this definition. We believe that tradition and good sense dictate that the property of being all-knowing be defined completely in terms of knowledge that something is the case. Given this understanding of 'all-knowing' we are confident no contradictions can be found."

The preacher said: "Are the gentlemen from the university sure they want to take this step? In the first place, the restriction they propose has the paradoxical implication that humans have kinds of knowledge God cannot have. Secondly, it attributes to God purely intellectual knowledge and only of a certain kind at that. Granted, this conception of God's knowledge may cohere well with the view of God put forth by theologians, but it does not accord with the ordinary religious believer's view of God. An ordinary believer tends to think of God as a super person who has many of the characteristics of ordinary people, but to a greater degree than ordinary persons. However, one characteristic of ordinary people is that of having knowledge how and knowledge by acquaintance. Thus, the price that the gentlemen from the university pay for avoiding contradiction either is paradoxical or a purely intellectual view of God that is not in keeping with the ordinary believer's ideas."

The smallest and youngest theologian said to the preacher, "We are aware of the implications but see no other way. Let the Preacher with No Name continue!"

"So be it! But I fear that the gentlemen's confidence in avoiding contradiction by this restriction is premature. Should I explain?" Without waiting for a reply, he went on, "Our distinguished listeners from the university continue to call me Preacher with No Name. For my purpose this is name enough. I am presently discoursing on contradictions in the concept of God. What I know when I am giving such a discourse can be known only by me. Consequently, God, as an all-knowing being, cannot exist, since God could not know what I know in knowing this. The gentlemen from the university might suppose otherwise. They might suppose that the idea expressed by the sentence 'I give a discourse on contradictions in the concept of God' is the same as the idea expressed by the sentence, 'The Preacher with No Name gives a discourse on contradictions in the concept of God.' Consequently, God could know what I know. But the two propositions are not the same. Although God could know the second, He could not know the first. What I know when I give such a discourse is not the impersonal kind of knowledge expressed by the sentence, 'The Preacher with No Name gives a discourse on contradictions in the concept of God.' I am proud and happy about my giving this. However, this is the knowledge expressed by 'I give a discourse on contradictions in the concept of God,' not 'The Preacher with No Name gives a sermon on contradictions in the concept of God.' My friends may be proud and happy about the Preacher with No Name giving this discourse. But only *I* can feel proud and happy of *my* giving this discourse, since giving the discourse is *my* action."

The tall and ungainly theologian said, "The Preacher with No Name wrongly assumes that the knowledge he brings up is knowledge that something is the case. I do not think it is. So God could exist and still be all-knowing in the sense of 'all-knowing' that we assume."

The preacher replied, "Very well, but your account commits you to paradoxes similar to the ones I pointed out earlier. First, an all-knowing being is supposed to have all knowledge that a non-all-knowing being has. But, on this account, I have knowledge that an all-knowing being does not have. Moreover, God is supposed to have at least all knowledge that humans have. But, on your account, I have knowledge that God could not have."

Then the red-faced, blond theologian spoke: "The Preacher with No Name makes a telling point. Let us admit that the sort of knowledge the Preacher with No Name has is 'knowledge that,' but that it is logically impossible for God to have this sort of 'knowledge that.' Let us say that a being is all-knowing so long as it has all the knowledge that it is logically possible for such a being to know. God could be all-knowing and yet not know what the Preacher with No Name knows."

The preacher sighed and said, "Alas, the problem with this solution, however, is that of the last. It is paradoxical to suppose that it is logically impossible for God to have knowledge that it is logically possible for some humans to have; it is paradoxical to suppose that it is logically impossible for an all-knowing being to have knowledge that it is logically possible for a human to have."

The five theologians spoke among themselves and then started to depart. The preacher saw this and exclaimed, "Do not go, my friends! I have many more contradictions to bring to the fore. You wanted me to justify my position and I have barely begun! I have only pointed out contradictions connected with God's being all-knowing. But there are many others connected with His being all-powerful and His being completely free." However, the theologians walked away from the Preacher with No Name and from the sea. The Preacher with No Name frowned and looked around. There were only a few people left in the crowd and most of these either seemed asleep or had blank looks on their faces.

"The theologians understood and left. Those who remain do not understand," he thought sadly. The Preacher with No Name bowed to what was left of the crowd and walked dejectedly along the coast to the next town. Yet it is said that some in the crowd who remained after the theologians had left did understand and were moved to God-Rejection. (From *The Book with No Name.*)

Mary, Mary, Quite Contrary

This is another story by the late Lois Grave which was found among her papers after her suicide. It is reprinted here by permission of Eastview State Press and her father, Clarence Grave.

Mary could hardly believe it. She was going to have dinner at Sir John Reardon's estate, and it was very likely that the Archdeacon of Carlisle, Reverend William Paley, would be there, since he had been a guest of Sir John's for over a week. After hearing his sermon a fortnight ago, she was most anxious to ask him some questions. That would only be possible if she could get away from the watchful eye of her father. The opportunity for doing so had seemed remote until two days ago, when her cousin Robert came for a visit.

"Dear Cousin Robert," said Mary when she had

the opportunity to see him alone. "I must ask a favor of you. It is terribly important, but I will understand if, given your moral scruples, you decide to decline. Nevertheless, I need not remind you of the numerous times I have helped you with your philosophical studies and with other sundry matters. Although I would never decline your future requests for help even if you should refuse me, I would henceforth accept them with a heavy heart and only out of a sense of duty."

So that Robert could not see the twinkle in her eye while she was making this speech, she turned away from him, and only faced him when she was sure she had a serious demeanor.

"My dear Mary, of course I will aid you as much as I can. You know that! You do not have to remind me of your help. What can I do?"

"I wish to confer with the Revered Paley when we dine at Sir John's tomorrow. Father is afraid that I will attempt to undermine his arguments and forbids me to pass anything more than the time of day with him. I need you, Robert, to distract my father's attention while I have the opportunity to discuss certain aspects of his position. I have one or two propositions that I would put to him," she said, her eyes flashing.

"Mary, I did not know that your request would be of this kind. But given my past intelligence of your character I am not surprised. You want me to help you to deceive your own father as well as refute the great William Paley, for refute him you surely will if you have the occasion! For shame, Mary Taylor! If your father finds out what has transpired, he will have nothing further to do with me and I will not be a welcome visitor to his house. This would be most undesirable."

"Robert, my dear, in the first place, I do not intend to refute Reverend Paley. I repeat, I only want to put one or two propositions to him. In any case, I deem it unlikely that my father will gain intelligence of our subterfuge if you exercise due caution and carry through my plan with understanding. However, if he does, I will accept all of the blame. It is well known in our family that Father is incapable of thinking ill of you and will naturally conjecture that I led you astray."

"Very well, my dear Cousin. Let me hear your plan. I will obey!" Robert laughed at the delight and mischievous genius in Mary's eyes as she revealed her plan. To him it seemed simple and brilliant. After dinner Robert was to suggest that Sir John show Mr. Taylor and him his pack of hunting dogs, which were reputedly the finest in the county. Mr. Taylor had expressed interest in seeing them for years. Mary would start off talking to Lady Reardon and other women but would slip away to the library where the Reverend had been working in the evenings. While pretending to look for a book, she would strike up a conversation and after a while put her propositions to him. Her father would never know, because she would ask Reverend Paley not to tell him. She saw no reason why he should refuse her request.

The first part of the plan worked beautifully. Mr. Taylor leaped at the opportunity to see Sir John's dogs, and Mary had no trouble escaping from her ladyship into the library. When she entered the room, she saw Reverend Paley smoking a pipe while seated at a large table covered with papers. He smiled amiably at her as she pulled volumes off the self and pretended to glance at their titles. Finally, she put the final stage of her plan into operation.

"Reverend Paley, I had the great privilege a fortnight ago of hearing you deliver a most edifying sermon."

"Really, my child? Did you enjoy it?"

"Oh, very much indeed! There were one or two points, however, that I had questions about. I wondered if you would spare me a few moments of your valuable time and satisfy my curiosity."

"Why, yes, my dear child. I dare say that my sermons are far less intelligible to the fairer sex, since I do use a considerable amount of logical reasoning," he said, leaning back in his chair. "Even some men profess not to understand me," he said smiling.

"Well," said Mary, speaking rapidly, "it is precisely the logical reasoning that concerns me. I have questions about the inferences you draw via an analogy. In your sermon you maintained that just as we can infer that a watch found on a heath has a designer, so we can infer that the universe has a Designer. This designer you designate as God."

"Yes, very simply stated that is my basic argument," said Reverend Paley in a patient tone of voice.

"You went on to say—and I believe this a correct quotation—'Every indication of contrivance, every manifestation of design, which existed in the watch, exists in the work of nature; with the difference, on the side of nature, of being greater and more, and that in a degree which exceeds all computation.' "

"I believe you quote me accurately," said Reverend Paley.

"My one question," said Mary, trying to control her voice but with only limited success, "is this: By what reasoning do you identify the Designer of the universe with God? God is incorporeal and created the universe out of nothing. But if one follows through on the analogy of the watch, the Designer would have to have a body and use preexisting material, since this is what an actual watchmaker does. My second, related question is why one is forced by the analogy to conclude that there is one designer. A watch is usually made by many intelligent beings. The argument proves some form of polytheism rather than monotheism. In short, my basic question is: Does not your argument in fact prove that God, as we commonly understand Him, does not exist?" Mary was about to continue when she perceived that the effects of her questions on the Reverend Paley were not what she had expected. She had imagined that he would either be amused or annoyed. She had even considered the remote possibility that he would not understand. But nothing in her imagination or experience had prepared her for what in fact happened. Reverend Paley started to rise from this chair, his face red with rage, and then fell back gasping for breath.

Beside herself with fright, Mary quickly obtained a glass of brandy and held it to his lips as he sipped it. In a few moments he seemed somewhat recovered and said: "My dear young lady, I am very sorry to have reacted in such a manner to your questions. You presented them so forcefully and without warning that I was quite justifiably shocked. I am not accustomed to young women raising difficulties with my argument. Does your fertile mind generate theories of this kind often?"

"Yes, I am afraid it does," she said quietly.

"I see. I believe that I am fully recovered now. Perhaps you are desirous of relating more of your theories to me."

"Sir, I think under the circumstances this would be most unwise. For . . ."

"No, I insist. Your theories are of vital interest to my work."

"Well," said Mary, going on in much a more subdued manner, "there is another point entirely. I believe that you and other thinkers who use similar arguments suppose that we judge an object to be an artifact, and thus that it is created, in terms of whether it serves some purpose."

"Yes, I believe you are correct," said the Reverend Paley.

"But does this accord with actual practice? In fact, does one not distinguish an artifact from a natural object by the evidence of the machinery and the materials from which the objects are made? Travelers in Africa and India, for example, decide whether something is a rock or a hand axe, not by determining if the object can serve a purpose, but by looking for those certain marks left by flaking tools and not produced by the weather."

"Yes, I take your point," he said slowly.

"Well," she said, "whatever these tests are, they do not apply to the universe. The universe does not meet these tests."

"Yes, my dear, but this hardly shows that the universe is not created," he said, appearing to be nearly recovered.

"Not with absolute certainty, of course. But I urge you to consider the probabilities, Reverend! We know that almost always when an object has certain peculiar marks on it, these have been left by a flaking tool and the like and, consequently, that the object is created. We also know that usually when an object does not meet these tests it is not a created object. Since the universe does not meet these tests it probably is not created!" Mary said in an excited voice. Catching herself, she said, "I am afraid I am getting carried away again. Please forgive me."

"Nonsense. I am quite all right now. However, I see a problem in your position. Don't you assume what you are out to prove by supposing that objects without marks are not created?"

"I have not assumed that the universe is not created; I inferred this from the evidence. According to the best evidence that we have, if some object is not made of certain material, does not have certain markings, and so on, it is usually not created. Such evidence could be mistaken, but it is the best we have to go on. Of course, we might change our minds if we could survey the entire universe. But we cannot. We must proceed on the evidence we have. Although the universe is unique, there is no reason to suppose in the light of our present evidence that this is relevant in judging whether it is created or not. We have no reason to suppose that it cannot be judged by the same criteria that we use to judge whether planets, rocks, and axes are created."

Reverend Paley smiled: "You are indeed a remarkable young woman. Frankly, one might to tempted to believe that the sort of mind you have is quite wasted in a woman's body. Some might go so far as to say that you should have been born a man, my dear. However, this would come dangerously close to saying that God made a mistake and this I cannot believe. At the moment I am afraid I do not see exactly how you fit into the divine economy, but I am quite confident that you do!"

"But Reverend Paley, what about the merits of my argument? Have I not shown that if one takes the analogy that you use seriously, then the Designer of the universe could make mistakes just as watchmakers do? And doesn't the last argument that I gave suggest that the universe is not created, and hence that a Designer does not exist? Yet you lapse back into . . ." She caught herself in time. Reverend Paley's face was growing red and his breath was again labored. She poured him another glass of brandy and held it to his lips.

"Please, my dear, perhaps you should go. It has been a very trying evening," he said, leaning back in his chair.

"Yes, of course. I would be very obliged to you if you did not provide my father with any intelligence of our conversation tonight. I fear he would be very angry at me, since he has forbidden me from discussing theology and philosophical topics. Indeed, sir, I came to you tonight expressly against my father wishes."

"I see. Very well, I will keep your secret, if you keep mine."

"Yours, Reverend Paley?"

"I wish you to promise me that you will never tell anyone what transpired here this evening. Will you agree to my request?"

"Yes," she said, and so saying left that room and hurried back to the drawing room, arriving just in time to meet her father, Robert, and Sir John coming in the other door.

"Sir John, you have a monstrous fine set of dogs. Strike me if they're not the best set I've seen in many years!" Mr. Taylor was saying.

"You are very kind to say so," said Sir John.

Robert was suddenly at Mary's side.

"Well?" he whispered.

Lowering her voice, she said, "Reverend Paley was not disposed to talk to me. I thank you very kindly nevertheless for your efforts on my behalf, Robert.

You were very manly and brave and I shall always remember it."

"Mary, my dear," said her father, "I trust you had a pleasant evening talking to Lady Reardon, your mother, and the rest of the women."

"I am sorry to report, Mr. Taylor, that your charming daughter disappeared shortly after you left and reappeared only at your return," said her ladyship.

"Indeed! Perhaps you would like to give an account of your activities, Mary?" said Mr. Taylor, looking very grave.

"Certainly," said Mary. "I was feeling unwell and thought a turn about the garden would be beneficial. While passing the library I noticed that Reverend Paley was working there. I had a strong inclination to stop and put certain propositions to him that were relevant to the validity of his philosophical theology." Mary paused. Mr. Taylor looked stricken. "However, I decided against this course of action, since you had explicitly warned me against it and, in any event, it seemed unkind to interrupt him in his most important work. Taking a pleasant walk about the garden, I returned refreshed and feeling quite myself," she said smiling sweetly. "I see," said Mr. Taylor, reassured. Mary glanced at her mother and was not sure whether she had guessed the truth.

"Mary, dear," Mrs. Taylor said, "please come to the piano and sing that lovely ballad you rendered so exquisitely last year for Sir John and Lady Reardon."

"Of course, Mother," said Mary.

The Death of Beneficent Ben

"Geez, Uncle Ben, ya look real bad," Eddie said that day after school. "Uncle Ben, are ya goin' be all right?" Eddie was real scared that Uncle Ben was going to kick off. He had lost a lot of weight and looked sort of pasty. The lump on his leg was about as big as a softball and although Beneficent Ben was suffering terribly, he never complained. "Eddie ol' boy, come here," he said. "We've been through a lot together, you an' me. I taught ya everythin' I know 'bout the con game an' ya gotta be pretty good at it! Your ol' Uncle Ben is damn proud of ya!"

"Oh, Ben, don't die!" Eddie said, and he started to bawl. "I ain't got nobody but you!" This sure was the truth! Since Eddie's ma and pa croaked when Eddie was a lad, Beneficent Ben was Eddie's pa, ma, teacher, and preacher. What Ben preached was not what most preachers preached at church on Sunday.

He hardly ever quoted the Good Book, and he never talked about Heaven or Hell or such things. But what he did say made pretty good sense. Sure Beneficent Ben was a con man, but he had a big heart and a feeling for what was right and wrong, and that's a damn sight better than most of those preachers.

"Eddie," he said, "Ya should never con anyone who can't 'ford it. There're plenty of suckers out there who're rich an' greedy. An' 30 percent of what ya get goes to the poor! 'Member, 30 percent!" Beneficent Ben was the best damn con man Eddie ever knew. Christ, he was the best damn con man in these parts! Give him a rich, greedy bastard and he'd milk him for all he was worth. He was so damn believable! So honest looking! Damn, he was good! But give him a poor, sick, widow lady and he'd give her his last nickel.

But Ben was dying. He told Eddie that day after school. He didn't want to go to the hospital because he was afraid of hospitals and such things, and anyhow, he said that he was saving money for Eddie's future—his Eddie, he'd call him. Well, ol' Ben died after a month of suffering. The last thing he said to Eddie was, "Be a good con man, Eddie, ol' boy! An' 'member, 30 percent!" Eddie stopped believing in God and such right after that. The way Eddie figured it, if God was good, he'd wouldn't have let Uncle Ben suffer so. If ol' God was so damned mighty, he'd have stopped it. But God is supposed to be good and mighty. So there ain't a God! Although Ben never said so in so many words, Eddie had come to guess that Ben thought that religion was a big con game and preachers were con artists. Eddie suspected that Ben was right. There ain't a God, but, damn, just think of the dough that the churches make by getting poor saps who think there is to contribute. And most of these churches don't even give 30 percent of what they take in to the poor! Even Beneficent Ben knew better than that! Years and years later, when Eddie was an old man, he thought back to his growing up with Beneficent Ben, to the old days with Subway Slim when he was working the good cons out of 'Frisco, to his broken marriage, to his granddaughter, Little Lois. He thought, "Hell, I only lov'd two people in my life: Beneficent Ben and Little Lois. Ben died horrible-like, an' thanks to her mother, Little Lois probably hates my guts now! He thought back to the last time he'd seen Little Lois. It was her seventh birthday and it was the last time Fast Eddie would ever be allowed to see his granddaughter.

"Tell me about Beneficent Ben again, Grandpa!" said Little Lois. Fast Eddie told her for the first time about Beneficent Ben's death while leaving out the most horrible details.

"I'm sorry, Grandpa!" she said. "Grandpa, why didn't God stop Ben's pain?"

Eddie couldn't bring himself to tell the truth. He said he didn't know. However, he said although God moves in "mysterious ways," he was sure there was a good reason for Ben's suffering. Little Lois's eyes grew wide and her little brow knitted together.

"Do you really believe that, Grandpa?" she said.

He hesitated for a moment and said: "No, Honey, I don't."

"Neither do I!"

Fast Eddie smiled at his little granddaughter. "She's sure a savvy kid!" he thought. "She should be a philosopher or somethin' like that when she grows up."

God for a Day!

Today was the day! Billy Eaton was so excited! He had prepared all week. He had made long lists of things that he would do. He had asked questions of everyone on the ward to help him decide what to put on the lists without letting on what they were for. Yesterday he had asked Nurse Johnson, who he considered pretty smart, "Johnson, if it was in your power to change the world and make it a better place, what would you do?"

Nurse Johnson looked at Billy with a professional eye. "Have you taken your medicine this morning, Billy?"

"Yes, I have. Come on, Johnson, what would you do?"

"Oh, I don't know," she said. "How much power would I have?" she asked, smiling.

"The sky's the limit!" he said, trying to suppress his excitement.

"Well, then, I would cure children of diseases of various kinds. I would stop war and famine. I would . . ." She stopped and looked at Billy. "Why are you asking me this question, Billy?"

"Just interested," Billy said, looking very sheepish.

"I don't believe you," said Nurse Johnson, moving on to the next ward as she gave Billy a playful slap on his rump.

He also asked Dr. White when he was making his rounds.

"Good morning, Dr. White," Billy said respectfully.

"Good morning, Billy," said Dr. White, sitting down beside Billy, whose several sheets of yellow paper were spread out on a table in the patients' lounge. "Aren't we busy this morning!" he said cheerily. "How are you feeling? Any bad dreams?"

"No. I haven't had any of those for several months."

"Good! Good! What about the voices? I believe you thought you were having conversations with President Lincoln several months ago."

"That's right, Doctor White. I also thought I was talking to old Sergeant Allen, my Marine Corps drill instructor. No, I haven't heard from either for some time now," he laughed good naturedly. "It must be that new medication you have me on."

"Yes, it has shown remarkable results in several clinical trials."

"By the way, Doctor White, to keep myself busy I am making a list of things to do to improve the world. So I want your opinion. If it was in your power to change the world and make it a better place, what would you do?"

"What do you mean 'in my power'? Do you mean with my present resources? These, as you know, are rather limited."

"No, I mean if you had all the resources there were! If you could do anything! Change anything! Fix anything!" Billy stopped when he noticed Dr. White looking at him intently.

"You mean if I were all-powerful?" asked Dr. White.

"Yeah, something like that," said Billy cautiously.

"Do you mean if I were God?"

"Yeah, I guess so," Billy said with a touch of annoyance in his voice.

"Billy, are you sure you are not hearing voices again?" asked Dr. White gently.

"No, honest, Doc!" Billy pleaded.

"I remember several months ago when you started asking questions about General Grant's Civil War campaigns. You lied and said you weren't hearing voices. You told us later that President Lincoln had asked you to take command of the Union Army from General Grant. We had quite a time getting you settled down. It would save a lot of time and trouble if you would tell me the truth now."

"No, Dr. White. There is nothing like that going on now," he said, looking Dr. White straight in the eye.

After Dr. White had gone, Billy went back to constructing his lists of things to do. "Dr. White was no help in making my list," he thought. "And he suspects something, too. But he doesn't know the whole truth."

Billy thought back to how it had started. He was having trouble going to sleep one night and without warning God began speaking to him. It was easy to speak to God, easier than speaking to the nurses or the other patients, with the possible exception of Lois. God told Billy that He would like Billy to become God for a day. God told him that he could make any changes he felt were needed, and if he did a good job, he might be able to continue a while longer. God said that Billy could take over on Tuesday. God was not sure when on Tuesday He would have Billy take charge, but He said that Billy should be prepared at any time. God for a day! Billy could hardly contain himself. He could not sleep for the rest of the night and the next morning he started to prepare himself. What good works he would do! What miracles he would achieve! What works of humanitarianism he would accomplish! At the end of his day of being God, the universe would be unrecognizable! It would be a place of joy and happiness instead of misery and gloom! Let Dr. White find out! It would be too late. Mental hospitals would be one of first things to go. Mentally ill people and mentally retarded people would be cured instantaneously and no others would be born or created. Sadistic drill instructors at Parris Island would have to go, too. He already had ten yellow pages of things he would do, and he knew that he had barely scratched the surface. Still, even if he did not do everything that should be done, he would make a big improvement.

After breakfast on Tuesday, when God had not yet put him in charge, Billy decided to visit Lois. He had not yet told her the news and he thought that this might be the time. He found Lois sitting on a bench under the big elm tree near the infirmary, reading a thick book. She smiled as she saw Billy approaching. "Hello, stranger!" she said. "Where have you been keeping yourself? I haven't seen you in over a week."

"Oh, Lois, I'm so excited! Wait 'til you hear what's going to happen today!"

Still smiling she looked tenderly at Billy.

"God is going to put me in charge today! I am going to be God for the day!" Billy said breathlessly.

Lois's smile faded and she said slowly, "Well, Billy, that is big news."

"I can do it, Lois. I've been preparing all week. I've made lists of things I will change and things I will improve. One of the first items on my list is to get rid of your depression."

"That's very sweet of you, Billy."

"Yes, wait 'til you see the things I'm going to do when I become God!" he said, pulling yellow sheets of paper from his pocket. "First, I'm . . ."

"Billy," Lois said gently, "I have a few questions I would like you to think about."

"Sure, Lois! You can be a big help to me when I become God. You have a terrific education, and there's nobody whose mind I admire more than yours. I want you to ask questions!"

"Billy, you say that you are going to change things and improve things when you become God. But why haven't they already been improved?"

Billy looked blank. "I don't understand what you mean."

"Well, if you become God, you will be all-powerful."

"Sure, Lois. Everyone knows that."

She went on, "So you will have the power to make improvements. You would also be all-good, so you will want to make them. Furthermore, you would be all-knowing, so you will know how to make them."

"Sure," said Billy, sitting down on the bench, still clutching the yellow sheets of paper.

"But, Billy, don't you see? Right now, before you become God, before you become all-powerful, all-good, all-knowing, the real God—the Being whose place you are taking—already exists. Why hasn't He made the improvements on your lists? Why hasn't He cured my depression and achieved all the other noble goals you have considered? Why are there any bad things that need improvement if God exists?"

Billy was stunned. Lois always asked great questions, but today she had outdone herself. "I don't know, Lois. Do you?"

"Let's consider some of the things on your list and see if we can come up with any answers."

"One thing I have on my list is to stop parents from abusing their children. Is your question, Lois, why didn't God do this long ago?"

"Yes, but some people think they have an answer. They say that if parents were prevented from abusing their children, this will be preventing God's creatures from exercising their free will. These people believe that a world with free will and child abuse is a better world than a world without both free will and and child abuse."

Billy thought for a moment and then said, "I think that is a dumb answer."

"Why?" asked Lois, placing her hands in her lap and leaning forward.

"Why? If I am God, I will make the world a place where people have free will and never abuse children and things like that. Why can't God do this? If people have free will, it does not mean they must do bad things. People in Heaven have free will and don't do bad things. Why do people in this life?"

"Do you think there is anything else wrong with appealing to free will?" Lois asked.

"Well, even if people choose to do bad things, God could prevent the bad consequences of what they do. If I fire a gun at someone intending to kill them, God could make the bullet miss its target or make the gun misfire. So I could have free will, choose to do evil, and yet not do evil," Billy said with great energy. Lois laughed despite herself.

"Let's forget about the free will argument for a while. You want to hear some of the other things on my list?" asked Billy.

"Please!"

"Well, when I become God, I will cure children of crippling diseases and of mental retardation. I will also prevent any more children from being born crippled or retarded. Now is your question, Lois, why hasn't God already done this?"

"That's right. Obviously appealing to free will would not help in these cases."

"Why not?" asked Billy.

"The evil is not brought about by human choice," said Lois as she got up and stretched.

"Oh! But how do they explain these evils?"

"One answer they give is that crippled and mentally retarded children are necessary for achieving a greater good. Having no such children would make things worse!"

Billy did not dismiss this idea out of hand. "Gosh, I guess that's possible," he said thoughtfully, "but it doesn't seem very likely. Anyway, there are all sorts of other things on my list that also have nothing to do with free will. It seems crazy to suppose that all of these evils—tornadoes, hurricanes, volcanic eruptions, mental illness, cancer—are necessary to some greater good."

"But couldn't these evils be important for building human character? After all, human beings do develop character by fighting against evil. All the things that you have just mentioned provide us with lots of character-building obstacles to overcome," Lois said.

Billy was not sure from the look on her face whether she was completely serious. "Oh, come on, Lois! God could build character without making mentally retarded children! Anyway, sometimes the evil is so great it crushes and destroys people. Look at what happened to me in the Corps, and remember I told you once about my Aunt Beth who had cancer. Well, . . ."

Lois held up her hand to stop Billy from telling the story about Aunt Beth that she had already heard many times.

"Yes, Billy, I agree," she said. "I just wanted to see how you would react."

"Are there any other ideas of why God has not already done the things on my list?" asked Billy.

"There are. But you might not like these any better," she said.

"Try me!"

"Suppose God is not all-powerful. Then He might not be able to bring about any improvement," she said, pretending to shield herself from Billy's forthcoming attack.

"What? God would have to be pretty weak! Some of the things that could make the world better even human beings could do. Who could worship a weak God like that?" he demanded in a loud voice.

"Suppose God is not all-good. Then He might not *want* to improve things!" she said.

Billy laughed. "Come on, Lois, be serious. By definition God is all-good."

"Yes, but perhaps not in our sense of 'good,' " she said, sitting down in her chair.

Billy thought this over for some time. "Yes, I see what you mean. But unless God is good in our sense, why should we worship Him? This doesn't mean, of course, that humans define 'good.' However, unless God was good in our sense, He would not be our moral ideal. My uncle Joe was good in his sense of 'good' but . . ."

"Enough, Billy!" Lois said emphatically. "Let's try to wrap this up. I have to go take my medication in a few minutes."

"Okay by me. I must confess I am a little confused. We have talked a lot, but what can we conclude? Anything?"

"Well, the question was why hasn't God already done the things on your list? We considered some answers and they all seem to be unsatisfactory."

"Where does that leave us?" asked Billy softly.

"There is one possibility, old friend, that I have not broached, although it seems like this is the time. Perhaps there is no God," Lois said, looking at Billy intently. "This would fairly well explain why the things on your list remain to be done. There is no God to do them."

"But God talked to . . . you mean I didn't really talk to God?"

"It is possible," said Lois, touching Billy's hand softly.

"Well, who did I talk to? That's what I'd like to know."

Lois said nothing and looked at Billy compassionately.

"So I won't become God today?"

"I think it's unlikely," said Lois.

As the hours of the day passed and he did not become God, Billy kept hoping that Lois was wrong. But when it became nine o'clock in the evening and nothing had happened, Billy had resigned himself. He was depressed for only a few moments. "What a great God I would have made," he thought sadly. "What works of humanitarianism I would have accomplished!"

He saw Dr. White making his evening rounds and

waved. "Well, Billy, how is your list coming along?" asked Dr. White.

Billy took several crumbled sheets of yellow paper out of his pocket and threw them in the waste paper basket. "Oh, I've given up on that, Doctor. Lois has convinced me that . . . never mind, I just don't think it is a good idea anymore. By the way, Doctor White, do you believe in God?"

"Why, yes, Billy I do," he said, rather startled.

"I don't!" exclaimed Billy, and he wondered if the doctor had ever considered the problems that he and Lois had discussed. "It's too bad you do," he said, waving goodbye to Dr. White and walking into the recreation room. Then he heard a deep, familiar voice speaking to him out of what seemed like eternity. "Are you ready, my son, to take over my work?"

"Knock off pretending to be God, Sergeant Allen! Get off the line!" Billy said. "I want to speak to President Lincoln."

The Free Will Improvement Project

As the Uno Star space shuttle moved slowly into the docking station at Summa, a female voice came over the intercom: "Passengers departing at Summa please stop at the main computer console for an I.D. check. On behalf of Captain Talo and the rest of the space crew, it has been our sincere pleasure to serve you. Remember, when you travel again in the Argon system, travel Uno, the fastest and safest space shuttle in the system. Those passengers continuing on to . . ."

Harry picked up his bag and walked toward the door. He was apprehensive to say the least. The idea of going off Planet M 789 was hard for him to get used to. Still, in order to get to do the sort of work he knew he was capable of doing, emigrating was absolutely necessary. Harry had left the general environs of Plainview to attend the university at Balsam some 100 kilometers away and, of course, he had made periodic visits to his father's mining camp in the high mountains on the other side of M 789. But he had never been off the planet before. In fact, few people in Plainview had. The only person he knew who actually had left was his old school chum Nicka Ta, who only last year had taken a position in the elite Division of Practical Philosophy of the Institute of Advanced Research on Summa, the largest planet in the Argon system. Frankly, he did not like leaving the comfortable world he knew and loved and traveling to Summa, several light years away, but the position of Director of Neurocomputer Research was one he could not refuse. After an I.D. check at the computer console, Harry started looking for Nicka, who had promised to meet him. She was not hard to spot. There she was, standing in the center of the lobby, all two meters-plus of her. Motionless in the sunlight with her deep purple skin, bright red eyes, majestic bearing, and flowing white robe, she looked like a queen ready to receive a diplomat. This fleeting impression of royalty was soon shattered. When she saw him, she beamed, bounded across the lobby in three graceful, loping strides, and practically swept Harry off his feet.

"Harry, Harry!" she cried, "how wonderful to see someone from home!"

"Nicka, you look wonderful! I gather from your radiant smile that things are going well for you at the Division of Practical Philosophy."

"Yes, my old friend, they are going well. We are doing very important work that might have great humanitarian applications. However, we need someone with your technical skills to complete some of our projects. You would do me a great honor to dine with me tonight and give me your expert opinion. I see tremendous possibilities of cooperation between your division and mine."

"Yes, Nicka, I would be delighted. What a splendid idea!"

On the way to her apartment, although Nicka talked gaily about her family, commented wryly on the politics and cultural climate of her new home, and recalled fondly her schools day with Harry, she said nothing about her present friends or personal life on Summa. In particular, she was strangely silent about her betrothed, Gunna Wa. When they finally arrived at her apartment, Harry ventured to say, "Nicka, I note with interest that you have not spoken a word about your forthcoming bonding with Gunna. Has something happened?"

Nicka looked away and said, "The Bonding Ceremony has been postponed indefinitely, and it is unlikely that it will ever take place."

"But why?"

"The story is long and complicated, Harry, and it is very much involved with the complex mores and culture of our people. The brief version is simply that in the Kumma W'ta scheme of things, after bonding the female is expected not to work, but to stay with her children. Steeped in this culture, Gunna and his parents were unable to see any other point of view. As you must surely suspect, I have other plans for my life. When I refused to agree to this arrangement, his parents withdrew the official offer of bonding, and negotiations between our two families broke down completely. I hasten to add that my parents have been splendid. They have supported me completely in my decisions. They are, of course, unusual—in fact, they are quite rare."

"Yes, I remember from our childhood you telling me long ago that you were raised as a nonbeliever in a society in which belief in many gods was the official religion."

" 'Oh, the number of Kummaitos is a thousand and one and their power is great! Let us follow their teachings throughout our lives! Let us dance as they danced in creating all existence! Let us live on the land and in the sea as they live! Let us bond together—male and female—and generate the Kumma W'ta without end!' " Nicka intoned rather sarcastically. "Yes, that is true, Harry. Nonbelievers or atheists are rare in our society—perhaps only 1 percent of the population. But they are well educated and organized."

"Is there no hope for you and Gunna?" Harry asked.

"It is extremely unlikely that we will be bonded. He agrees with his parents, and even if he did not, he would obey them. A son going against his parents' wishes on decisions concerning bonding is virtually unheard of."

"But can there be no one else?" Harry asked.

"In principle, yes. I could be bonded with some other nonbeliever beside Gunna. No one outside of the small class of nonbelievers would do, of course. But the prohibitions against females working outside the home is very strong even among the nonbelievers. Even if a son had no scruples, his parents probably would and, as I have already mentioned, sons do not go against their parents' wishes on this matter."

"I see."

"There is a further complication in my case. Because of my father's work I was raised on Planet M 789, far away from our home, among human beings.

Consequently, I simply do not know many Kumma W'ta males of my age, let alone of a nonreligious persuasion. Here on Summa there is, of course, a small Kumma W'ta enclave. But it is very conservative. As far as I have been able to determine, there are no other nonbelievers."

"Is it really that bad?" Harry asked.

"Yes, I am afraid so. But I did not invite you home to tell you my personal problems. Please come in the kitchen, Harry! While I prepare the meal I will fill you in on some of my ideas."

As Harry watched, Nicka glided around the kitchen. Like a dancer moving to music, she sliced, diced, and mixed the various ingredients that constitute a typical Kumma W'ta meal. As she worked, she told Harry of the mission of the DPP and her job there. "The main function of the Division of Practical Philosophy is to come up with ideas that benefit humanity," she said, deftly cutting a large, purple fruit into small pieces. "We try to anticipate problems in the ethical, political, and philosophical implementation of these. Although our division does not itself judge the technical feasibility of implementing the ideas—we do not have the technical knowledge to do so—we work closely with other divisions of the Institute to do precisely this. The final recommendations of whether to implement the ideas are made by the Board of Directors of the Institute. If they recommend implementations, then they must sell the idea to the High Council of the Galactic Federation. Despite political obstacles it is surprising how often they are successful," she said as she placed a large bowl into the oven. "I am working in what is half jokingly called the 'Free Will Improvement Project' of our division, and we have come up with some interesting ideas. We had very much hoped that your division would be willing to test their technical feasibility and develop methods of implementation insofar as this would involve neurocomputer technology," she said. "We believe they are quite revolutionary and could change our society."

"The Free Will Improvement Project? Please, explain!" Harry said.

"Well, do you remember the free will defense from your introduction to philosophy class at the university? The project is closely related to some ideas connected with it."

"That sounds like theology!" Harry said in surprise. "What is an atheist like you doing in such a project?"

"Our meal is prepared!" she said. "While we eat I shall tell you."

Nicka served a salad of translucent red and yellow vegetables that Harry had never seen before, let alone tasted. Nicka explained that they had been imported from her home planet and were not available on M 789, and that she had become acquainted with them only on moving to Summa.

After they ate the salad she said: "The free will defense, Harry, as you may recall, is a defense against the problem of evil: How can God, who is all-good, all-knowing, and all-powerful allow moral evil; that is, how can He allow human beings to exercise their free choice in order to do evil? The free will defense argues that moral evil cannot be blamed on God, since it is the result of free human choice; consequently, human beings are responsible for moral evil. Despite the possibility of misuse, God gave humans the ability to make free choices because a world with free choice is more desirable than a world without it."

"Yes, I recall the basic idea," Harry said. "But is this defense also found in the religion of the Kumma W'ta? Your people do not believe in a being that is all-good, all-powerful, and all-knowing?"

"Yes, it is," she said. "For there is also a problem of evil in our religion. For although the Kummaitos are not all-powerful, they are extremely powerful, and they are all-good and all-knowing. Our holy books teach that the Kummaitos could have created the Kumma W'ta always to do good, but they rejected this option for the same reason that your God is supposed to have rejected it."

"I see. Although I recall the defense, I am a little vague on the objections against it," Harry said, leaning back in his chair.

"I will get to these directly, for it is the objections that are crucial in generating the so-called improvements in free will," she said. "But let me serve the next course."

So saying, she sprang lightly to her feet and disappeared into the kitchen, reappearing a moment later with a crescent-shaped loaf of bread and a dish of what appeared to be greenish-purple cheese. "This, my friend, is a cheese made from the milk of the giant mountain sheep of my home planet. It is considered a delicacy by the Kumma W'ta and with practice may even be enjoyed by humans."

"But, to return to our discussion, the objections to the defense are many. Some critics have argued that the price for free will is too high and that morally sensitive persons would not suppose that a world with free will—given its gross misuse—is better on balance than a world without it. Others have argued that although a world with unlimited free will is better than a world with no free will, a world with limited free will would be a better world still. For example, imagine a world in which there was no free will to commit mass murder, but where there was free will in all other cases. The question, then, is why did God not create this world."

Harry found that the strangely colored cheese was quite wonderful and had already finished two pieces of bread thickly spread with it. Nicka again sprang to her feet and disappeared into the kitchen, this time reappearing carrying a steaming bowl of a thick vegetable stew with a pungent and spicy odor. "This dish," she announced, "my mother taught me to cook when I was a girl in Plainview. Although all the ingredients are available from the local environs of Plainview, they are virtually unknown to humans." Harry had to admit that he had not seen any of the ingredients before.

Sliding into her chair she continued the philosophical discussion: "Another objection is that moral agents could have been created with free will but with a propensity to do good. It is logically possible that humans have free will, that is, that their choices are not determined by causal laws, and yet that they have a very strong tendency to perform morally correct actions. If so, although there would be no causal necessity in humans choosing one way rather than another, it would be very unlikely that they would choose to do what is morally wrong. Such a world, it would seem, would have great advantages from the believer's point of view, for it would have free will but very few moral evils. It would seem that an all-good and very powerful creator or creators would want to and could create such a world. The question is, then, why our actual world is not like this."

While eating his stew Harry had a thought.

"Nicka, I wondered if there might be problem with the last idea. Might it be said that it makes no sense to say that moral agents have a built-in desire to do good, since the desire to do good can be learned and developed only through experience?"

"Yes, Harry, some people have raised this objection, but it has little merit. It does not seem to be part of what one means by 'doing good' that it can be learned and developed. Surely powerful creators as the Kummaitos could create moral agents with a built-in desire to do good. An all-powerful being such as your own God would have no problem. One need not be limited to human or Kumma W'ta psychology as it is presently constituted. Furthermore, it is not obvious that in order to have a world in which people possess a tendency to do good there must be an innate desire to do good. Although I don't believe the Kummaitos exist, I am convinced that if they did, they could have created a world in which there are moral agents who have a strong tendency to do good that is not innate but learned and developed."

Harry could not remember when he had enjoyed such a delicious meal, and leaned back in his chair contentedly. "There is more to come, Harry!" she said, springing to her feet again. This time she emerged from the kitchen with a large bowl of the purple fruit Harry had seen her preparing earlier. She kneeled in front of Harry and offered him the bowl saying: "Eat of the sacred fruit of the Kummaitos, Oh honored guest! May you live long and grow wise! May you dance with the Kummaitos in eternity!" Nicka arose laughing. "I haven't done that in years! The offering of the sacred fruit was a rare but memorable ceremony of my childhood. You should be honored, Harry. This is only the second time I have made the offering to a human."

Harry was honored and even touched. To his unsophisticated palate the sacred fruit did indeed taste like the fruit of the gods, somewhat like a cross between pineapple and strawberries but much sweeter. Settled again in her chair Nicka proceeded, "There are other problems with the defense. But let me mention what I believe is one of the most important ones. Some have argued that the defense is really irrelevant."

"How so?" asked Harry.

"Well, what does it mean to say that people do no moral evil? Does it mean that they are morally perfect in the sense that they always make the morally correct choice, or that they perform no actions having morally objectionable consequences? Suppose it is true that God could not have created a world in which human beings never choose to do the wrong thing. It would not follow that He could not have made a world in which there are no actions that have morally objectionable consequences. A moral agent could then be less than morally perfect and yet never do anything with morally objectionable consequences. Presumably God could have constructed natural laws in such a way that any attempt by a moral agent to do some morally objectionable act would end in failure; that is, the consequences of the act would not be morally objectionable. In this world a mass murderer would choose to kill millions but he would be unsuccessful. However, in such a world one's moral choices are not causally determined. It follows that free will is compatible with no action ever having morally objectionable consequences."

"This seems like a very powerful argument," said Harry. "In fact, all of the objections you have raised seem difficult to answer. But what I don't understand yet is how this fits into your research project. In particular, I don't see how my work at the Neurocomputer Division is relevant."

"Ah, now we come to the interesting part! Please move into the living room." So saying, Nicka vanished into the kitchen and materialized an instant later carry two glasses of a light green liquid. She gave Harry a glass and offered a toast. "To the forthcoming cooperation between the Division of Practical Philosophy and the Neurocomputer Division! What God and the Kummaitos have failed to achieve let our cooperation accomplish!"

"Nicka, what is that toast supposed to mean?" asked Harry.

"Just this. I propose to investigate the possibility of doing some of the things God and the Kummaitos have not done. Could we devise moral agents that have free will but a tendency to do good? Could we devise moral agents who have free will but of a more limited nature than we do now; for example, who would not be free to commit mass murder? Could we arrange things in such a way that even if moral agents acted with evil intent their actions would not have evil consequences? My group would explore the moral, political, and philosophical ramifications of doing this, and your group would investigate the technical feasibility. Well, what do you think?"

"Why do you want to do this, Nicka? To prove the nonexistence of God or the Kummaitos?" asked Harry, finishing his drink.

"Being successful would not be irrelevant to this goal, of course. If we were successful, this would show that nonsupernatural beings could improve free will and, consequently, that supernatural beings certainly could. Whether it would be desirable is another question, but I believe good reasons could be given to show that it would be. Since it is possible and desirable and yet not done, it is likely that neither God nor the Kummaitos exist, for if they did exist, they would have already have done it. However, this is my own personal opinion and it is not essential to being committed to the project."

Harry did not say anything but seemed to be deep in thought. Nicka continued. "I recall from our youth —the trip to the circus and your story about seeing Jesus while attached to the Religious Experience Machine are ingrained in my memory—that you were a believer. I can well understand how you might not share my goal," she said quietly. "But I repeat that this is my personal goal and is not the official one."

"No, I am not a believer anymore, Nicka. I read some of the God-Free literature and holographically transmitted speeches of the Preacher with No Name. I gave up my belief long ago in light of what I read and heard. However, I might have serious reservations about playing God," Harry said gravely. "I understand all too well now what you mean by improving on free will."

"Let me remind you, dear friend, that no implementation would even be proposed until the feasibility—ethically and politically—is exhaustively investigated. Then it would be implemented on an experimental basis and carefully monitored. What you call 'playing God' has been done for centuries. Operations to remove cataracts and cure club feet, the cure of mental illness by chemical therapy, the elimination of diseases by genetic engineering were all called 'playing God' at the time they were proposed. The difference between these things and 'improving free will' is only a matter of degree."

"Perhaps," said Harry, without much assurance in his voice.

"There are ethical and political issues, to be sure. This is my department and these will be considered at length, I assure you. But for now let me pick your brain, Harry! Are these ideas technically feasible? What about limiting free will without ruling it out entirely? What about allowing people to decide but preventing harmful consequences of their actions? Suppose that there were some actions so monstrously wrong that it would be a better world if people could not decide to do them. People would have free will in all other matters. For example, suppose that it would be a better world if people were not allowed to commit genocide. Or suppose people could choose genocide, but their action could be prevented from having harmful results? Off the top of your technical head, do you see any ways of limiting free will to prevent this without limiting it in other ways? Can you think of ways to allow free will but limit its consequences?

After a few moments of thought Harry said, "In principle there should be no problem. Although the work is still in the experimental stage, neurological implants have already been used to monitor the behavior of psychotic killers and prevent them from killing. The implants are hooked up to the police computer network so that any intention to kill on the part of an implantee would be instantly relayed to the authorities so preventive action could be taken before the person acts. Implants have also been used on alcoholics. Here the implant is not hooked to a computer, but is constructed in such a way that it directly inhibits the person from drinking by, for example, causing the implantee to become nauseated when he or she thinks of drinking alcohol."

"Could these be adapted to our purposes?" Nicka asked excitedly.

"Oh yes, I think so. There are many technical problems to be worked out, of course. In the alcoholic case, the implant causes an adverse physiological reaction in the implantee. It does not affect thought directly. But there is no reason in principle why this could not be done. For example, an implant could be constructed that would prevent anyone from even thinking of committing genocide. Or if this is deemed too restrictive, it could be constructed in such a way that it would prevent anyone from deciding to do any action that has a high probability, say 70 percent or more, of being genocidal. The implant would be hooked to a computer that would estimate the probabilities given the available information. There are many computers that could be programmed to perform such tasks."

"Sometimes genocide is not intended, but is an unintended consequence of many microactions. Is there any way of handling this problem?" Nicka asked.

"Yes, if we knew what the likelihood was that some microaction could lead to genocide in combination with other actions. Then we could have implants that would prevent people from thinking of these actions (if and only if others also thought of them) and the probability of genocide occurring as a side effect of these actions was high."

"What about the possibility of creating moral agents who have a tendency to do good but who could do evil?"

"Do you mean via genetic engineering or brain implants or . . . ?"

"Whichever!" Nicka said as she poured Harry another drink.

"Well, genetic engineering is a little out of my line,"

he continued. "As far as I know, no one has yet developed moral agents via genetic engineering of that kind. But there has been recent interesting work at some primate laboratories. For example, kongs, the giant apes who were designed for mining labor, were especially created to be nonaggressive. Kongs still fight when provoked, but it takes a great deal to induce them to. I see no reason why similarly genetically constructed nonaggressive hominids could not also be made. However, with respect to brain implants, which are more in my line, there would be no problem in principle. Implants have already been used to inhibit but not completely repress certain kinds of behavior, for example, sexual behavior. Sexual criminals with sexual inhibitor implants commit sexual crimes at a rate approximately 80 percent less than those without the implants. These implants work not by preventing ideas of aggressive sexual acts such as rape, but by lowering the desire to do such acts. Immoral behavior is more complex than sexual behavior, but in principle it is capable of a similar inhibition. A person who does some immoral act often knows that it is immoral but does it anyway. The implant might be designed to inhibit but not entirely suppress the tendency to go against what one believes is wrong."

"But, Harry, what if the person has no developed sense of morality? Suppose he or she thinks genocide is morally permissible?" said Nicka in a concerned tone of voice.

Leaning back in his chair and savoring his drink, Harry said, "In that case, the implant would have to be constructed differently. It could be designed to inhibit any behavior, even behavior that the implantee did not suppose was wrong. It could also be designed to make the implantee believe that genocide is wrong, although he or she did not previously suppose so, and to inhibit genocidal behavior. The implantee would still have a choice. He or she could choose to do wrong. The implantee would just be given a different set of values. He or she would be free to reject these. I hasten to add that no actual studies have been done in this precise area, but there are analogous areas of investigation. For example, there are studies where mathematical implants have been used that give implantees mathematical knowledge and induce them to use it. They can reject such knowledge and inducement, but it is difficult."

"Harry, I think you have said enough to convince me that you are ideally suited to be involved in testing the technical feasibility of some of the ideas in the Free Will Improvement Project. The question is whether you want to."

"Yes, I do, Nicka. It sounds exciting and important. I still have reservations about playing God, but that is your department. But it is late and I have to go," he said, getting to his feet. "Your hospitality was more than I anticipated or deserved. Your Kumma W'ta dinner was a thing of beauty. Thank you, Nicka! When I get settled I will invite you to dinner, and you can sit and watch me do all of the work!"

"You are most welcome, Oh honored guest!" she said, bowing gracefully. "Of course, I will drive you to your new apartment, Harry. But before that I would like to say one more thing about playing God or, as the Kumma W'ta say, believing you are a Kummaito. If God existed, God would play God; that is, He would make all of the ethical decisions that we must make if He does not. I believe we can not only improve upon free will but improve upon the way things are decided. If God exists, He set up free will in His way without consulting us to see if His creatures approve and without any feedback from them. When we play God, we will not be so arbitrary. We will consult with those whom our decisions affect and propose alternatives for their consideration."

In the days and months that followed, Harry thought about what Nicka had said and about his dinner with her. "She is truly a remarkable and brilliant woman," he thought many times. "But she is not human. She is a nonbelieving female Kumma W'ta who has gone against the mores of her people—the rarest of creatures—and because of it, I am afraid, a very lonely one. Fortunately, she has her work."

The cooperation between the Free Will Improvement Project and the Neurocomputer Division was close and creative over the next two years. Harry and his colleagues worked at a feverish pitch to develop a new brain implant that would inhibit approximately 80 percent of the desire to commit violent crimes. Working in cooperation not only with the FWIP, but also with a new private research company, Implants Unlimited, on Summa's sister planet, Radum, Harry and his colleagues developed an implant that did not inhibit the desire for violence, but managed to prevent many of its worst effects. An implant introduced into a would-be perpetrator of a violent crime would alert the proposed victim of the perpetrator's impending act as well as register the intention on the police computer. Given this warning, potential victims could often take preventive action, and the police would know who was about to commit the crime and on many occasions prevent it. Computer simulation studies suggested that this implant would eliminate many of the harmful effects of violent crimes and prevent others.

Meanwhile the work of Nicka and her colleague was proceeding swiftly. They dealt mainly with two important ethical issues. First, how could implants be prevented from being misused to monitor an individual's private thoughts and desires? The police should not have access to all of an individual's private mental life, yet they should be able to obtain knowledge of people's intentions if this knowledge would help to prevent the commission of a violent crime. What constitutes legitimate police information? When is an individual's privacy infringed? Nicka and her group worked closely with legal philosophers, law enforcement officers, and civil rights groups in developing alternative proposals, and, in a democratic manner, finally arrived at one that was acceptable and workable to all parties. The computer program screened all information going to the police and no one—not even the designer of the program—had access to illegitimate information. Indeed, the computer did not keep illegitimately defined information in its memory, but erased it after it was screened. The other problem had to do with the implantees. Who should have the implants? Everyone? Only former criminals? Should it be voluntary? How could people be assured that the implants would not make them robots or that the implant would not report their every thought?

After long deliberation with community leaders, Nicka and her group decided on an informational and educational campaign to be followed by public hearings. Then a community with a serious crime problem would vote on whether they wanted implants. If the majority wanted them, then the implants would be required for everyone in the community. After two years the community could reassess the experiment and if they were unhappy with the implants, they would be removed. What was learned from this social experiment could be used in improving implant design and community implementation in future cases.

The proposal was approved by the Board of Directors of the Institute. Given the high crime wave in many parts of the Federation, there was little problem in selling the idea to the Council of the Galactic Federation. Because Plainview was the home city of the two principle investigators, it was designated as the target city. After six months of public information, education campaigns, and numerous public hearings, the proposal was put to a vote. It was passed by a wide margin by the citizens of Plainview and was to be implemented in six months. It was decided that the new implants—detectoplants—from Implants Unlimited on Radum would be used primarily for economic reasons: they were cheap and easy to put into place. It was indeed a time for rejoicing at DPP, the Neurocomputer Institute, and Implants Unlimited.

Nicka decided to throw a party. The Head of the Research Division of Implants Unlimited, Gordon Blackburn—someone Harry had not yet met—was arriving from Radum on the space shuttle to join in the festivities, and Harry went to meet him. When Harry arrived at the spaceport a little late, he immediately went to the information desk and had Gordon Blackburn paged. "Mr. Gordon Blackburn, arriving passenger from Radum, please meet your party at the information desk!" As soon as the announcement came over the loudspeaker, Harry heard a deep voice behind him saying, "I assume you are Harry English." Harry turned and looking up at a purple-skinned, red-eyed giant—a Kumma W'ta—attired in human apparel. "I am Gordon Blackburn," he said, grinning broadly. "I see that you are surprised that I am a Kumma W'ta. I suppose I should have warned you. It's the human name, I guess. I was raised by humans and took their name."

"I see. Yes, Gordon, you did give me a little start." As they walked to Harry's ground car, Harry asked, "Is it unusual for a Kumma W'ta to be raised by human parents?"

"Very. In fact, I have heard of only one other case. Both of my parents were killed when I was a baby and I was raised by human friends of my parents who had no children of their own. They loved me as their own and I adored them," said Gordon as he moved down the ramp in that gliding fluid walk so characteristic of the Kumma W'ta.

"Do you not know the Kumma W'ta culture and customs then?"

"My adoptive parents thought I should know my cultural heritage and endeavored to teach me the basic customs, myths, and legends of my people. I learned the language and in recent years have actually started to read the rich literature of the Kumma W'ta. For fun I sometimes use my Kumma W'ta name, which is An'o Beha. However, most of my friends are human and to a large extent I am more human in my orientation than I am Kumma W'ta."

Harry thought carefully and then said cautiously, "Are you bonded?"

"Unfortunately not. I certainly wanted to be. There are problems in my case."

"I see," he said although he did not completely.

"Yes, I learned the myths and customs of the Kumma W'ta and found them beautiful and moving poetry. However, I certainly don't believe them. The legend of the amphibious Kummaitos—the thousand-and-one dancing divine beings of our religion—taken literally is preposterous. Unfortunately, that kind of sentiment is extremely rare in the Kumma W'ta. My human parents' atheism influenced me to a certain extent, of course. The literature of the God-Free movement was always available in our home and I actually heard the Preacher with No Name speak on several occasions when I was a lad. He made a a deep impression on me. To add to my problems, since I was raised by humans, I know few Kumma W'ta females, and the ones I do know seem—how shall I say it—tradition-bound."

"I assume you are aware that our hostess tonight, Nicka Ta, is a Kumma W'ta," said Harry, trying to sound causal.

"No, I did not know," said Gordon in a peculiar tone of voice.

"Yes, and you may be interested to know that she is not bonded and is, like you, a nonbeliever. There is one more thing you should know about her. She is brilliant and is set on continuing her work if and when she becomes bonded. Because of this commitment, her proposed bonding with one Gunna Wa has been indefinitely postponed and without doubt will never take place."

"But can she cook?" Gordon asked.

Harry turned in shock to Gordon, who burst out laughing. "I learned to have a sense of humor from my human parents."

"As a matter of fact she can," Harry said, also laughing.

"Well, in that case I will suggest a bonding contract be initiated tonight. This time I am serious. I would be prepared to move to Summa."

"But is this not rushing things a bit?" asked Harry, rather surprised.

"No, I think not. But we shall see what Nicka's reaction is," Gordon said and spoke not another word until they arrived at Nicka's apartment.

Nicka threw open the door and was taken aback to see Harry and the giant Kumma W'ta. Harry said simply, "This is Gordon Blackburn, also known as An'o Beha, the Director of Research at Implants Unlimited, a nonbeliever who was raised by humans and thinks the tenets of the Kumma W'ta religion merely beautiful poetry and Kumma W'ta females too tradition-bound and he would be willing to move to Summa."

If Nicka grasped everything Harry said, her face revealed nothing. Bowing low she said quietly, "Welcome to my home, honored guest, An'o Beha from Radum! May your stay be blessed by the thousand-and-one Kummaitos! Would An'o Beha consider dancing with me the dance of the Kummaitos as a preliminary to the sacred bonding ceremony?"

Gordon also bowed low. "Gracious and graceful hostess, Nicka Ta, you honor me with your hospitality! May the thousand-and-one Kummaitos bless your home! Let the dance of the Kummaitos preliminary to the sacred bonding ceremony begin! I await moving to the sacred music with you at my side!"

The Satanic Curses

I went to bed late and for some reason had difficulty falling asleep. When I finally did I had an amazing dream. Satan paid me a visit. In my dream he wasn't such a bad guy, although he was not terribly convincing. I dreamed that I was sitting at a desk in a dark office. In the background, ragtime was playing while lights from a neon sign reflected on the walls. There was a soft knock on my door. "Come in," I said. The door slowly opened and standing in the doorway was a rotund gentleman wearing a three-piece suit, patent leather shoes, and a monocle. He had a goatee, carried a walking stick, and wore a wide-brimmed fedora pulled at a jaunty angle over one eye. Bowing slightly when he saw me, he strode into the room.

"Allow me to present myself," he said, bowing low and sweeping off his hat in one fluid motion. "I am Satan."

"I don't believe you," I said.

"Do you mean that you don't believe I am Satan, or that you don't believe Satan exists?" he asked as he slid into the chair directly opposite from me. Smiling, he revealed a set of large yellow teeth.

"I don't believe in Satan, and even if I did, I certainly would not believe that you are he," I said, trying to speak in a modulated tone.

"But my dear chap, to make philosophical points you refer to Satan very often in your lectures. Moreover, you wrote to a character in Dostoyevsky's novel *The Brothers Karamazov* who was a devoted disciple of a person whom I visited in the novel. Don't you recall that I visited Ivan Karamazov? If I can visit him in his delirium, surely I can visit you in your dream! How can you say you don't believe in me? As far as my appearance goes, I can well imagine that you had supposed that Satan would look different. However, I take on many forms. Today I travel as a European gentleman; tomorrow, who knows? Did I not appear in a similar form to Ivan Karamazov? What can I do to make you believe me?"

"Well," I said, "I assume you can produce horns and a tail."

"Why, of course! But why are you so conventional, dear boy? Do think that Satan must be like the myths about him? However, if horns and a tail will convince you, then by all means . . ." So saying he brushed back his thick, wavy hair and exposed two small horns. He was about to lower his trousers when I stopped him.

"That will not be necessary," I said quickly. "I would like to know why you have come to visit me, and then I want you to respond to the criticisms I have raised about your explanatory value. I suspect that your answers would convince me of your identity more than your physical appearance would."

"Fair enough!" my visitor said enthusiastically. "I have come to meet the person who said that 'the Satan hypothesis' does not answer the question why there is natural evil in the world." He pulled thoughtfully on his goatee as he waited for my reply.

"It is true that I do not believe Satan is a very good explanation of natural evil. Do you?"

"Why, of course I do, my good fellow! If I did not think so, my existence would be very dreary," he said, emphasizing his point with a forward thrust of his walking stick.

"Let us be sure we understand that we are talking about the same thing," I said, leaning back in my chair and beginning to feel more at ease. "As I understand it, natural evil is all the evil in the world that cannot be attributed to human beings' deliberate and intentional actions. This kind of evil is not only brought about by disease, earthquakes, and other so-called natural processes, but is also produced accidentally, unintentionally, and negligently by human action and inaction."

"Yes, yes!" he said impatiently. "Get on with it!"

"It is not implausible to suppose that most of the evil in the world is natural in this sense. A significant portion of the harmful events in the world are brought about by human actors who either did not know the consequences of their actions or did not believe that what they were doing was wrong. Thus misplaced idealism, ignorance, short-sightedness, and circumstances that induce people to act cruelly to one another out of what seems to them commendable motives surely account for many of the horrors of the past and present. Add to these wrongs disease and natural disasters such as earthquakes, famine, drought, and tidal waves, and the large majority of the bad things in the world are probably accounted for."

"So why doesn't my existence account for this?" he asked in an almost wounded tone of voice.

"There are several problems. As you noted only a few moments ago, you are supposed to take on various bodily forms. However, as I understand it, you are basically a disembodied conscious entity having once been a fallen angel of God. Is that correct?"

"Yes, what of it?" he asked sharply.

"In the first place, experience shows that consciousness is always causally dependent on physical organisms. All of our evidence indicates that consciousness is always associated in a body. Indeed, we have no clear counter instances—cases in which there is consciousness and no body. This does not show that consciousness could not be independent of bodily processes, but it does render such an idea very unlikely. Thus, we have evidence that makes your existence unlikely." I went on quickly, warming to the task, "Moreover, if Satan does take on bodily form, one would expect that there would be reliable eyewitness reports of satanic creatures with superhuman powers. That no such reports seem to exist provides some evidence against the satanic hypothesis. That you are appearing to me in a dream proves my point. If you are real, wake me and appear to me in reality."

"Sophistry and humbug!" he shouted, his face flushing in anger.

Trying to ignore his rage I went on. "There are other problems as well. The hypothesis of Satan fails to explain why good people are not inflicted with more evil than bad people. One would expect that if certain laws of nature were designed by Satan to bring about evil, more morally good human beings would be struck down than ones who were evil. Satan is portrayed as giving certain privileges to those who follow his evil ideals, but no such pattern is discernible. Evil people are no better rewarded than good people by natural happenings."

"If I had my way, I would reward the bad and punish the good" he said earnestly. "But HE will not let me! HE interferes with my plans! HE is always in my way!" he said, his voice breaking with emotion.

"Really? I don't believe a word of it. I thought that God gave Satan free will just as he gave human beings free will. The idea is that a world with free will, including a world where *you* have free will, would be a better world, all things considered, than a world without it. To prevent you from working your system of rewards and punishments would be to intervene with your free will. You must be mistaken that God interferes with your plans.

"You are distorting things," he mumbled.

I pressed on. "Another problem with the Satan hypothesis is that one would have expected you to perform miracles, to interfere in the natural course of events in order to perform evil works. There are many incidents in the history of the human race in which if some human action had been stopped, the human race would have been worse off. Suppose Dr. Salk, the inventor of the serum to prevent infantile paralysis, had been struck down by your intervention before he completed his work. The human race would surely have been worse off than it is. Yet there was no satanic intervention. Certainly you have the power to intervene, since any being that can create laws governing disease and tidal waves could strike down a scientific researcher on the verge of a discovery."

"If I had it to do over again, I would have caused Salk to have a heart attack. At the time of his discovery, it did not seem that important," he said rather apologetically.

"Nonsense! At the time everyone knew it was a major medical breakthrough. But in any case, there are thousands of other medical and scientific discoveries that had wonderful humanitarian consequences that you could have prevented," I said, my voice rising.

"Satan works, as does God, in mysterious ways," he said, lowering his voice and casting his eyes down.

"You certainly do! What you do really makes very little sense!" I said with growing confidence. As I spoke I noticed a change in my visitor's appearance. He seemed to grow slowly transparent and I began to be able to see through him.

"One more thing," I said. "There are certain natural evils that we have every reason to suppose are not caused by you. These are evils that are caused by free human actions that are based on nonculpable ignorance rather than evil intent. Since they are the result of free human action, they are not caused by Satan; since they are the result of nonculpable ignorance, they cannot be blamed on human beings."

My visitor made no response except to fidget in his chair.

"There is also this point. One must ask who tends to repudiate this belief in you and who does not. There is good reason to suppose that belief in you tends to be repudiated by people who are the best educated and the most intelligent and tends to be held by people who are less well educated and less intelligent. We know that religious conservatives tend to believe in you more than those who are religious liberals. We also have good reason to suppose that there is an inverse correlation between degree of religious conservatism and degree of education and intelligence. Thus, it is likely that there is an inverse correlation between degree of belief in Satan and degree of education and intelligence. Furthermore, since education and scientific sophistication are highly correlated, one can infer that there is probably an inverse correlation between degree of belief in Satan and the level of scientific education achieved."

My visitor was now scarcely visible, although I could hear him softly cursing me under his breath. As I rose to administer the coup de grace, he vanished from my dream. I remained alone in the dark room. The ragtime music was still playing and the neon lights were still reflected on the wall. I felt a little disappointed, because I had one other argument to present. I would have liked to say to him, "Even if one grants that your existence is not an improbable hypothesis, one wonders why God does not help the victims of natural disasters, i.e., the victims of your indirect actions. Since these victims are often unable to help themselves, one would have thought that a loving God would help them if He could. Indeed, even other human beings would seem to have an obligation to help if they could. That a person is not responsible for some evil does not mean that he or she has no responsibility to aid the victims of the evil. Yet God does not come to aid the victims of natural disaster: they die in horrible ways in great agony and suffering. He seems then to be either immoral or less powerful than those humans who do aid the victims of natural disasters."

My dream ended, but I do hope that I dream of Satan again. There are a few more arguments that I thought of once I awoke that I would like to present to him.

Sergeant Allen and Professor Hick

Sergeant Gene Allen walked straight to Captain Bonner's desk and snapped smartly to attention. "Sergeant Allen reporting, Sir!" he barked.

"At ease, Sergeant," said Captain Bonner, glancing over Allen's record folder without looking up. Bonner was impressed. Fifteen years in the Corps, paramarine, combat in Iwo Jima, Okinawa, and Korea, the silver star, several purple hearts, astonishing proficiency scores, hand-to-hand combat instructor, and now drill instructor at Parris Island. When Bonner looked up he saw a tall, well-built man whose picture should have been displayed on Marine Corps recruiting posters. From his blond crew cut to his spit-shined shoes, he was every inch a Marine.

"Sergeant Allen, I will get right to the heart of the matter. Up to this point your record in the Corps has been exemplary. But there have been some recent worrisome reports about your methods as a D.I. As you know, drill instructors at Parris Island must train young Marines in the finest tradition of the Corps. But there is a fine line between rigorous training and overzealousness. There have been reports . . ."

"Before the Captain outlines the charges against me, may I ask a question?" Sergeant Allen said.

"Very well," said Captain Bonner.

"What is the goal of our training at Parris Island, Captain?" said Sergeant Allen, shifting his swagger stick to his other hand.

"Why, you know that as well as I do: to make good Marines," said Captain Bonner with a little irritation in his voice.

"Yes, Sir, I know that. But what makes a good Marine? That's the question. I have a theory about this, and I have been trying to put it into practice since I became a D.I."

"What's your theory, Sergeant?" asked Captain Bonner.

"Well, Sir, I think that the key to being a good Marine is character, and that the training that the recruits receive here at Parris Island should build character."

"That is an interesting way of looking at it, Sergeant. But . . ."

"The way I see it, Sir, is that in order to built character the recruits have to be challenged and in fact made to suffer."

* * *

Bobby Larson and Joe Goldstein became the best of friends after their adventures in the Canadian Rockies over the Christmas Holidays and Joe's visit to

Bobby's home in New York during the between-semester break. Joe made a big hit with Bobby's mother and sister and in general the two young men got along famously. They also decided to take a philosophy course together. The course they chose was taught by a visiting professor, John Hick, and was called PH 209, the philosophy of religion. Joe, who seemed to know something about Professor Hick, said that he was a famous philosopher of religion and one of the leading advocates of a particular solution to the problem of evil called the Soul-Making Defense in the literature.

"The Soul-Making Defense? What's that?" asked Bobby.

"That's what I hope to find out by taking the course. But, roughly, I think it is the idea that God allows evil in the world as a way of building character. If God makes things too easy for us, we will not be challenged and would have weak characters. Get it?"

"Yeah, I think so. But I want to hear the details."

* * *

"Yes, Sergeant, I understand completely what you are saying. The Corps has always thought that the training should be tough and that this training is important to molding the esprit de corps that makes the Marines a proud fighting unit. Your theory in terms of character building is certainly in that tradition and in fact puts the whole idea in nice perspective. However, . . ."

"Thank you, Sir. But my point is that given this goal of character building, a D.I. has got to be tough. The recruits might complain, but it is for their own good and ultimately for the good of the Corps. Captain, I guess I just want to get that point squared away before any complaints are detailed."

* * *

Bobby and Joe were not disappointed with the course. Professor Hick surveyed the major problems in the philosophy of religion in a way that was both illuminating and fair. The high point for the two friends was a discussion of the problem of evil and in particular Professor Hick's soul-making solution to it. Professor Hick explained that the problem of evil was a serious obstacle to belief in God. Since God was all-good, He would want to prevent evil, and since He was all-powerful, He could prevent evil. So why is there evil? Hick explained that this was the traditional problem of evil. He favored one answer to the problem. Professor Hick put it this way in a lecture that stayed with Bobby for a long time:

> In creating the world God did not create a hedonistic paradise, but a place to make souls. Rational agents freely choose to develop certain valuable moral traits of character and to know and to love God. In order to do this they must be free to make mistakes and consequently to cause evil. This freedom thus accounts for the moral evil in the world. Moreover, in order to develop moral and spiritual character there must be a struggle and obstacles to overcome. In a world without suffering, natural calamities, disease, and the like, there would be no obstacles and no struggle, consequently there would be no soul-making. This account, then, also explains natural evil. Since soul-making is of unsurpassed value, its value outweighs any moral or natural evil that results from or is a necessary means to it.

* * *

"Very well, Sergeant. Before I get to the details of the complaints I would like to make a few general comments," said Captain Bonner, leaning back in his chair. "Your theory of character-building is valid only to a point. If one is too tough with our young recruits, they will break. In such cases, either they have to be discharged or they go over the hill or even physically attack their D.I.s. The Corps has recognized this for some time—although we have not followed good common sense in carrying this idea through as much as we should have. So, being tough is not always for the recruits' own good and it's not always for the good of the Corps. I am not suggesting that in your case mistreating recruits is a rationalization. I sincerely believe that you think that you were doing it for the good of your recruits despite clear evidence to the contrary. But, however sincere you were, your methods are excessive even by Marine Corps standards. One doesn't injure recruits to build character, Sergeant Allen."

Picking up a piece of paper from his desk he said, "Sergeant Allen, the details of the complaints against you are these. On June 24 you marched a detail of men in 105-degree weather for eight hours without rest and without water. The last hour of the march was done on the double. At the end you forced each man to do a hundred push-ups with a full fieldpack. Although several of your men complained of dizzy spells, you ignored them. Three of your men, Privates Kantowitz, Evans, and Bergin, were hospitalized with heat exhaustion, and Private Eaton had a mental breakdown and had to be discharged. I believe he is still mentally ill. On July 13 . . ."

* * *

"You know, Bobby, Hick's theory really is weird. It does not make a lot of sense. In fact, the more I think about it, the more bizarre it becomes," said Joe as they left the Dunster House dining room.

"What do you mean?" asked Bobby, munching on an apple.

"Well, according to Hick, the big justification of natural evil is that it provides hardships that make soul. Right? But there are plenty of evils to overcome without floods, disease, and stuff. Since the evil brought about by human beings—moral evil—provides a lot of material for soul-making, natural evil seems unnecessary. You see what I mean? We don't need natural evil, Bobby!"

"Yeah, but doesn't Hick have an answer to that argument? Didn't Hick say in last week's lecture that if there were not more evils than seemed necessary, deep sympathy and compassion would be impossible? I think he says something like that in his book, too," said Bobby, leafing through the text he was carrying. "Yeah, here it is. He says that unless human suffering seems pointless there would be no 'organized relief and sacrificial help and service.' "

The two friends reached their room and Bobby sprawled on his bed while Joe stretched out on the couch. "Yeah, I understand what he is saying, but does it hold water? I don't think so. Hick seems to be saying that people cannot show compassion to someone who is suffering unless they believe that the suffering is not necessary to build character. That's crap, Bobby! Listen, I bet my mom and dad felt great compassion for my suffering when they punished me, even though they believed the suffering was necessary to correct my misbehavior and indirectly my character. Hey, if you include suffering that is justified not just in terms of character development but in terms of other purposes, you get lots of compassion!"

"I think you're right," said Bobby. "My sister, Susan, worked as a nurse's aid last summer. She really identified with one patient who was suffering because of an operation that was absolutely necessary to restore her health. I don't think that nurses always show more compassion for patients whose suffering is for no good reason."

"But even if they did, it does not have to be," Joe said. "Hey, if God had wanted to, He could have created us in such a way that we showed compassion to all suffering beings whether we believed that their suffering was character-building or not!"

* * *

"Those are the complaints, Sergeant. Do you deny any of the charges?"

"No, Sir. I did all of those things. But I understood myself to be doing something good. Captain, could I say something about why I did those things?" asked Sergeant Allen.

"Yes, go on."

"Well, Sir, I sort of guessed that some of my men would break down and get sick and even that some might have to be sent to the hospital and then discharged. But the way I looked at it, Sir, is that if they cracked, they did not belong in Corps in the first place. Also, I tried to simulate combat conditions as much as possible. When you're out in the boondocks you don't rest. How can we teach our men what it is like in combat without being combat-tough at Parris Island? It doesn't make sense, Sir."

"Is that all, Sergeant?"

"No, Sir, there's one more thing. When a D.I. is real tough on his men it makes the men look out for each other more. They take extra special care of each other to compensate for what you called excessive methods. I bet, Sir, that I had the most closely knit platoon in Parris Island just because the men hated me so."

"Your observations are not borne out by the evidence, I am afraid. We have no reason to suppose that Marine fighting ability, esprit de corps, proficiency under combat conditions, and the like are a function of how much they hated their D.I. Nor in order to get men ready for combat do you have to injure and abuse them. Sergeant, I am recommending that a court martial hearing be convened. That will be all."

"Yes, Sir!" said Sergeant Allen as he snapped to attention, did an about face, and marched smartly out of the office.

Captain Bonner sighed deeply. "Some of these hard-ass sergeants! They think they are God! Perhaps the Corps would be better off without any of them."

* * *

The discussion continued the next night. Bobby's mother and her new friend, Dr. Beneke, were in town, and they invited Joe and Bobby to dinner at Grendel's Den. Dr. Beneke brought his daughter, Jennifer, a Boston University student. Bobby and Joe told Dr. Beneke, Mrs. Larson, and Jennifer about the course they were taking from Professor Hick and about the soul-making defense for the problem of evil. Although Mrs. Larson and Dr. Beneke contributed to the discussion, Jennifer hardly said a word as the two young men regaled them with their theories. Finally, Ann Larson said, "Why, I believe Jennifer took a course in philosophy of religion last semester. Am I right, Jennifer?"

"Yes, I did. It was wonderful!" she said as she lowered her eyes.

"Did you consider the soul-making defense?" asked Bobby.

"Yes, we did," said Jennifer.

"What did you think of it?" Joe asked.

"Well," said Jennifer, opening her eyes very wide and smiling brightly, "I agree with what Joe and Bobby are saying, but perhaps Hick is making a normative point misleadingly expressed as a factual one. Perhaps his point is that although humans sometimes show great compassion for suffering that is necessary for character building, their compassion should never be as great as in cases where the suffering is not necessary."

Joe and Bobby looked at each other and then back at Jennifer with new interest.

"Yet why should one accept this normative claim?" said Dr. Beneke.

"Oh, I don't think you should!" she said. "Our professor used this example. Mrs. Jones would never have developed the discipline to become a great writer if she had not been confined to her bed for many years with a heart ailment. Why should our compassion be less for Mrs. Jones's suffering than for Mrs. Smith's, who had a similar ailment and suffering and yet developed no character traits because of them? If we had been the nurse of Mrs. Jones and

Mrs. Smith and could have seen into the future, should we have given less care to Mrs. Jones than Mrs. Smith? This certainly seems wrong!"

"What is your professor's name at BU?" asked Dr. Beneke.

"Michael Martin," she said.

"Really? I met him at a party last year when I was in town. Afterward we had an interesting correspondence. He got me to see that I was really an atheist. I had no idea you were taking his class. He probably did not realize you were my daughter because we have different last names."

"Isn't your name Beneke?" asked Bobby.

"No," said Jennifer. "Fred is my step-father. My last name is Goldsmith."

"You said you are an atheist, Dr. Beneke?" asked Bobby.

"Yes, I am."

"I guess I am agnostic," said Bobby.

Dr. Beneke smiled broadly. "Well, here we go again! Bobby, I bet that I can convince you that you are an atheist just like Jennifer's Professor Martin convinced me!" Bobby saw his mother and Dr. Beneke smile at each other and Bobby had the feeling that as his new father Dr. Beneke probably would have lots of time to convince him.

Epilogue

God-Free at Last!

When the Preacher with No Name arrived at the northern forests he rested. He was spent and although he realized there was much work to be done, others would have to take it up and carry it on. His day was done. As he recently said, "Let them that are brave cultivate my seed! Let them that have ears hear my message!" Whether the brave would act and those with ears would hear remained to be seen. He drank from a cool stream, then sat on a log and looked northward up a green valley. He thought back to his brief ministry: the Doctrine of Nonbelief, the few minds he had opened, the many enemies he had created, the crowds he had addressed, the Sermon by the Sea, the Gospel of God-Free. Images flashed before his mind and even odors and sounds were recalled from his memory. He also recollected the pain, the disappointment, and the frustration. Was it really worth it? Sometimes he had grave doubts. Yet at other times he firmly believed that if only one person rejected belief in God because of his teaching, his ministry would be worthwhile. He hardly ever allowed himself to speculate on what the world would be like if most people did not believe in God. Today he thought he would indulge himself. He lay in a flowery meadow looking up at the clouds.

"What would things be like," he thought, "if belief in God were eliminated but other factors came to the fore? Could things well be unchanged? It is much easier to say what would not happen, or at least what need not happen, if the Doctrine of Nonbelief became widely accepted." He turned on his side just in time to see a squirrel run up an elm tree. After a while he continued his reverie. "There would not necessarily be any deterioration of moral standards, since there is no reason to think that nonbelievers have a lower moral character than believers," he thought. "Should one anticipate a decline in religion or church attendance in a society of nonbelievers?" he asked himself. "Certainly. But the extent to be expected is not clear. Religion is possible without belief in God, even with disbelief in God. Indeed, some of my critics have actually accused me of starting an atheistic religion!"

He laughed out loud at the very idea, then thought some more: "It is not only possible, it is likely that some people would continue to attend theistic religious services and to be members of theistic churches even if they did not believe. To some people church membership meets important social needs, and to others religious ceremonies have significant aesthetic value. The teachings of theistic religions can provide moral insights to nonbelieving participants. Indeed, I infer from the comments of people I have spoken to that some who have heard me speak were in fact members of churches and yet agreed with me."

The Preacher paused, then thought: "Would not nonbelievers control the seats of power and try to prevent the theistic minority from practicing their religion? Although this unfortunate situation could come to pass in a society that was virtually God-Free, there is no necessity that it would. There can be complete religious freedom for theists in a society in which the vast majority are God-Free."

The Preacher with No Name turned over onto his stomach and put a long piece of grass in his mouth. "But what would likely be some of the actual changes? Surely, the more obvious symbols and trappings of our present theistic society would fade away and disappear—everything from religious holidays to the use of expressions of God in oaths and exclamations. Theistic-based morality would be believed by few and this in turn would affect our views on moral education. Although people would find some moral guidance in the Holy Word, books such as the Bible would be read critically and would no longer be thought of as divinely inspired. Theistic religious leaders would no longer be looked to for moral guidance unless they had moral insights that did not purport to be based on revelation."

He actually started to become excited when he speculated: "If the Doctrine of Nonbelief became the dominant view throughout the world, one would predict vast changes in many different areas. There would probably be fewer wars and less violence than there is now. If the goal of God-Free was realized throughout the world, one would anticipate the secularization even of societies where religious fundamentalism is now a way of life. This in turn would bring about profound political changes."

His thoughts came down from the clouds to reality: "What am I talking about? The goal of God-Free will not become widespread in the immediate future. My travels throughout this land should have convinced me that there is good reason to suppose that theistic religions, especially of the fundamentalist variety, are gaining ground. Perhaps," he thought, "the most I can venture to hope is that my ministry will make a small contribution to helping to stem the tide."

He got up, swung the pack onto his back, and headed north. "Will there ever be a day when people can say with joy in their heart, 'God-Free! God-Free at last!' " he wondered. He realized that he would never know. (From *The Book with No Name*.)